THE SOVEREIGN ROSE
OF MORBID LORE

For McKenzie —
I hope you enjoy my first
published novel

Trinidad Mateo R.

A Novel

By

 TREE STORY

ISBN 978-1-64559-523-6 (Paperback)
ISBN 978-1-64559-524-3 (Digital)

Covenant Books, Inc.
11661 Hwy 707
Murrells Inlet, SC 29576
www.covenantbooks.com

To the Lord
To my family,
And to anyone who has ever supported me in my own personal quest to pursue my dreams. I thank you kindly; with all of my love and gratitude. From the bottom of my heart, in perpetuity.

Acknowledgements

For the Lord
For myself
For my family,
For my father, and his memory;
Departed, beloved, and never forgotten,
always in our thoughts;
fondly with heartfelt remembrance.

*"I never gave up on my own dreams because
I always believed in myself.
Only then could they be realized"*
                              ~ Tree Story

Chapter 1

Rising, the Rose, Said of Risen

*I*n omnia paratus: prepared for all things, all things change, and we must change with them. From whence I came, and to whence I shall return. One day, in the distant future; bright-colored and cultivated with hedges, as well as flowerbeds, including the irksome animals that will also be some of my greatest adversaries and affiliates in life, even the paranormal influences that will also help guide me through the broil and accolades of the most difficult pilgrimage; preferably with a statelier, royal, dignified, and majestic title that will also help reveal and dissect the introspective soul of an aesthetically pleasing flower.

Befitting: that was the habituated botany of the earth's surface and the unhabituated roses of the tremulous landscape that were ambulating on it with their thoughts and with their own personal stems. With their own personal memorandum and with their own personal ideals, as well as the adored and equally unadored day-dreamers of the ever-expanding hypothesis, including the focalized and defocalized gardeners of the earth's atmospheric flower beds; levitating, from here to the futuristic resemblance of the most demanding orientation, order, as well as thought-provocation.

Exacting: planted, watered, and raised; just below the clouds and above the integrity of the verdant hawthorns. Dendritic: all of them, as seen from the most distant depths of outer space, within, amidst, and beyond the stars of the world's floral beauty; herbaceous, woody, as well as blossomy, but those were the sovereign expectations of the figurative, standard-bearer that came with an otherworldly, godly or ungodly, celestial morbidity.

Metamorphosing, dispersing a flower's love for the world, as well as the facial features, including the functions and the conjunctive adverbs of the physical body as it pertained to the separate parts and elements that constituted the extraordinariness of the disparate composite.

Conceivably, that was the paradox of the male and female flowers, sundered or unsundered, but always blended in together, monotonously; he or she or it was traumatized by the prospect of an uninhabitable future.

Terminate or interminable, emotionally and intensely. Bravely: that was the protagonist, with or without a moniker. For now, you can call the aforementioned entity Innominate or Incognito. Either way he, she, or it didn't really care because it was always trenchant, adaptive, and unsparing, with a remarkably biting penetration, but not unchangingly.

Sententious: that's when we found out that "he" had a sharp, stentorian, treble excrescence about him, excited about the possibility of his own fulfillment. Otherwise known as the thorny, spiny, prickly descendants from a place called—The Flowerbeds of Elevated, Heavenly Clouds, said to be brazen, as well as valorous in the most likable state of fantasy.

Inwardly, that was the expert (said of whom, what, when, where, or why, nobody really knew the reasons why), but that's just because he was, and that's just the way it was. Inherently, with a worldview of the globe, as well as the real estate and global properties of the earth's terrain—by, from, which, and it was always constituted.

Subconsciously, in this case it was *he* or *his*, maybe even *him*, or *whom*. Nevertheless, those were the inner makings that were extruded and extracted from The Lore of Life's Lessons, death as well as his own personal self-examination.

That in itself was called *introspection*, as a counterpoint; that outside of itself was called *extrospection*, erecting the great debate about alliance, synonyms, as well as antonyms, fracturing the comparative analysis of comparison, as well as contradiction.

Flourishing or unprosperous: repetitive but still trying to blossom and always recycled; annually or biennially, preserving and confirming their own existence while undergoing and transforming themselves with a specific change in form and nature.

Inconceivably: that was the transmutation of the botany, reconfiguring itself with an amazing, carefully estimated precision that would help euthanize the common belief of the earth's impossibility. Set aside from the gossamers, as well as the marshy swamps of such high praise, including the remonstrance of commendation in the finest hours of their lives.

Separate from reality: that was the comprehensible stage of the understood mutation. Transpicuous, when everything else was still possible, and there was no such thing as impossible.

Ever-restless, the earth was still anxious, heavily swayed from the time it was created, but so was the moonlight, as well as the red line of red roses, in a long line of sight, rustling about the grand ole paradise of the northern lights by the stairway to glory, where he felt the love of every rose that has ever died before him.

Down below, much closer to the earth's meridian. Apprehensively, said of the earth's surface, prosperous or deathly in the countable degrees of heaven and earth.

As a personal observation: Eloquent or unmentionable in the flesh; dead or alive in the morning of the celebrated torches. Those were the rudimentary plants of the exterior glen that were also sensitized by the ghostly sounds of the evening shade; configured and reconfigured by the presence of the nightmarish poltergeists.

Sleepless or wakeless, nameless or keepsake; through the demonical eidolons, fuming with nostrils the size of ozone holes, blown up, by, through, and with the eruptions of the world's red-hot volcanos, referred from the study of their infernal burnings.

Hot-tempered: those were the hellish surroundings for the untitled, pseudonymous, torpedos, as well as the erotic demigoddess, for which he could only dream about. This was, and would be, the hardest journey in the history of flower-patterned, peregrinations.

Sent forth, awkwardly, that was the natural course of his, hers, and everyone else's life; when the botanical protagonists were suddenly departing from their parent types, reformatted with an incredible resonance of stupor, as well as an incredible resonance of enslavement, not to exclude the possibilities or the inner workings of their own entrapment, just as much as the inner workings of their own volunteerism.

Denied or accepted, of or relating to the word *aeonian*.

Gestating, lively or deathless, for the longest period of time, slowly from the womb of the earth's fertility, connected to the same, original, umbilical cords of the word—*macabre*.

Brilliant or foolhardy, that was the defunctive way of reasoning, responding to, and resulting in a much more tragic way of thinking; for the main nouns of the alternative glen (said of a person, place, or a thing); equally opulent, but still ravishing, and always subordinate; by, through, and with the startling nature of the word *morbidity*.

Earthly, miserly, appalled, and of course, weeping.

Repining, fretfully, in regards to the tellurians of the earth when it was still bacciferous; and when it was still capable of producing more melancholic storms the size of megacosms.

Experimental or intentionally, as well as the unencompassed islands of the universe, with wild imaginations and tropical trees than pictured berries, as well as the vegetation and brain stimulation of its own creation.

Inaugural: those were the heartwarming crops of a little red rose that were grown from the marl of the great western plains and fronts.

From here until the celestial seeds of tomorrow: Hemmed or unhemmed, those were the seams that remained unseamed. Scarred, from the dirty works of the most colorful artistes, with an eye-catching cough; bloodied with hammerheads of broken records and revolution, as well as the dirtiest securities of the earth's illusions; where all of the hearty, stout, and robust species of the world were about to bear their offspring, creating one of the greatest tragedies the world has ever known.

Down home, over yonder, in any way, or in any manner.

Over here, over there, overall, they were the earthlings, sequentially, amalgamated with all the miens, as well as the semblance and analogies of Mother Nature herself. Clashing, babbling, expressing loudly, the discordance of the opposing forces, said of the fires that were burning in the chimneys of hyperbole, as well as friction, plus the clanging of his own genuineness and guesswork.

Colliding in the credibility of oil and water: earsplitting, as well as the plausibility of their own realism, causing a similar explosion, and an even greater backlash in the standard structure of the universe, that would help redefine the meaning of the word *amalgamation.*

Lamenting: that was the reverberation of the earth's howling sounds, until the end of days, when all activity on the earth settled again, and the caterwauling of the felines could be restored, but only through the argute (cleverness) of rutting time; when all of the hymns of heaven could recall the outcry of squawking memories with a keening, esoteric lifespan.

More expansive, developing fetuses that resembled the inception of exorbitant hyperbole, embellished by the same symbolical cords of the little red muddled roses, as well as the integrity of the same botanical names and heads, even the zoologists that were equally but separately perplexed by the mutated life forms in the current state of affairs.

Clangorous, ear-piercing, finely spun with flimsy, insubstantial cobwebs by the threads of spiders, spinning their own webs of riddles, as well as their own booklets of metallic fiddle-faddle, with or without the fiddles of the fiddlers that were colluding, even preying, but always gloating on the rooftops of the world's most encompassed gales.

That's where I first fell in love with the articulate roses of the world's floral beauty.

Excogitating: those were the scenarios of life and death that were also floating in the air; cerebrating, forming, negotiating with the filament of confusion and conception, from where he stands, to the floral bulbs of delivery.

That was the crime, the sin said of my own personal virtues.

Screeching: that was the chaos, penetrating, vigorously. *Artfully: I was snipped, cleanly, without any blood drops or evidence that a heinous crime was committed, without any chemicals or toxic material; without any lunar intervention or atmospheric resistance to help stop, intervene, and prevent one of the most inane acts in the backdrop of the atrocious prophecy, puerile deed, with or without any kind of clue.*

Perceptive, I was grasping, driveling at the realization of wither and no wither. That's when I was introduced to the story of my story, ascending from the depths of my own deep contemplation—deadly, weening, but always phobic, especially at the steepest point of the most suppositional peak.

Raised, I was formed and solidified, sculpted from the aeration of the earth's surface, where I was first welcomed to the abhorrent forests of humanity by the way of a blithering, ghostly, ancient painter that was also pert but always polishing and grooming the bristles of the painter's brush.

Newly formed, with trifling matters, as well as a frippery of his own frivolity: Frothing, but not from the mouth. Spuming, but not from the hair follicles of his own intellect, or the brain waves from The Valley of Barefaced, Deafening Minutia. Yet there was still a place called The Valley of Flummery and Nonsense (complete idiocy and/or foolish humbug); *and they were always evolving, just as I was always wondering, thinking, and deciding what to do about my first impressions of them, myself, as well as the rest of the world.*

Whereto, wherefrom, and whereupon: I was always able to articulate my first words, actions, and even phrases in life, as well as my first thoughts with a gaudy, hard-driven flash of showy, but not always garish clothing and accessories.

Quantifying my own propositions: somewhere in the morning of a brand new future, or somewhere in the past of an old dying chronicle that has been lost in time, but right now I am somewhere in the present; walking strangely, against the wind, and against the probability of my own prosperity; blowing indications that I have been bred with an introspective soul, as well as a morbid way of thinking.

Classifying styles: somewhere in the ornaments of life, against The Wind Tunnels of My Own Autonomous Corporates, unincorporated by the darkness of the ostentatious morale. I was attracted to the classifi-cation of gloomy morbidity, and I can recall my very first word being "sovereign."

That was the first and foremost memory of my upbringing, mulling over the traditions of the specified frameworks that were also molding, as well as the environmentalists that were also cogitating over the blackened ecology.

Educational, that was my first unit of language, the one that I learned while I was still sketching my feelings amongst the trees, as well as the central location of my own heart, relating to my heart-whole exis-tence, near the symphony of The Twin River of Echoes, where they were all shared with the rest of the world, and I was able to perform my first choir of opinions; without a maestro, and without an actual person to attest for my own personal performance.

Contributory, I lent the painter my own personal euphemisms about genes as well as chromosomes, about seeds as well as embryos, about life as well as death, about peregrine birds as well as every other type of insect imaginable, about all of the other life-forms that the basis and premise of life had to offer the world in general, not to mention my own heritage.

Still, I was looking for a first and last name (preferably one that was not so anonymous, but much more bold and courageous), *including the alterations of life and death that would also help constitute my interstellar expressions.*

My thoughts, disguised by the ghastly cryptograms of time endur-ing eons.

Euphemistically challenged, I was introspectively morbid, heavily influenced, glom, motivated by the authoritative seeds of parental princi-ples, governed by a correct and reliable inference of the world's dictionary; said of words, as well as their cumbersome meanings.

Stellar: *I was lithe, pliant. Clumsy, flexible, but still contradict-ing myself, bending regularly. Lightly built, I was feisty, truculent, even obstreperous, and blandly urbane, in the metaphorical categories of life, such as love, luck, and even prediction, just as much as the diction of bad news and bad luck, spinning the symbolic wheels of my own fortunes but always prefaced by the brakes, and the breaks of my own misfortunes: nonstop, round the clock.*

More descriptively, I was gracefully slender in my figure, suave, lean, but somewhat tough and mean; in my personal demeanor and in my personal prattling approach.

That was the context of the mind-set, when the body was dictated by the functions that exceeded the parameters of my own otherworldly, personal knowledge about anything, and everything in life that was ever made meaningful or impertinent.

Thinking: inside and outside of the box. Orally, I was intellectually situated (of, at, or) occurring between the stars. Amongst the smallest units of life and amongst the biggest issues the world had to offer, including my own personal love to be potentate.

Rationalizing my own beginnings, from the dawn of civilization to the hydrogen bubble of the most earthly ballerina that was about to perform on the dance floor, built with the tools of my own stolid morbidity, but designed with an interactive, superfluous metaphor that would make me fall in love with her, or scare me to death.

Lustrous, wondrous: that was her worldliness. Overawed: she was nacreous, the mother of pearl, the mirror image of the universal terror, as well as the great-granddaughter of the world's pageantry, contradicted by the blemishes of her own beauty and horror.

Ruminating: she was duplicated, laced with colorless shoes and color-filled vituperation that would one day make her the femme fatale of my own introspective journey.

Replete: she was drawn, with a porcelain pencil; castigating, with an odorless spirit; brightening the stars of the future that were also imploding. Some from the origin of her ideate, others from the likelihood of her posterity, the rest from cardiac arrest, and the intensity of their own respective Illuminati, secretly killing the jest of the most guesstimated skeptics—twisting, turning, giggling, facetiously.

Adroitly, she spun around the dance floor with the sounds of things, eerily, with all sorts of stuff; oddly, with just as many inquests. Bemused by all sorts of questions, like what, when, where, how, or why she was even there in the first place?

Verbally abusive, we all had a purpose in life, and hers was combative, always ready to fight the most contumelious enemies of the mordacious belligerence, but that was the worst side of her.

Accompanied, physically and metaphysically, by the same masculine and feminine alliance of the scathing protagonist. Commonly referred to—The Connotation of Vitriolic roses, with a Specialized Fragrance of Cognoscente.

Consciously, she was the virtuous companion of the world that he cared about, more than anyone ever imagined. Piteously: that was a common side effect of human emotion, devastating the kindheartedness of his spiritual mind-set, existing somewhere else. For example, on the other side of the singular horizon, solely but not privately.

When he dies, he will think of her again, always in his thoughts, somewhere near, following him to the edge of the world's whispers, and all of its jaunty personification.

Biting in her style, as well as her overtone. Invective: she was denunciating, setting the tone for more emotive obstructions. Of life as well as death. All of which were about to come, cowing, humiliating, expressing her own litotes, scaring the most brutish men the world has ever known and weren't nearly as bellicose as she was.

Twirling: she lit her ribbons with flammable gases, exploding into the commorancy of time and space, with a chemical imbalance, modifying the orbit of the planet—ceaselessly, in the morning of her own imagery.

Inherently; that was my lineage, reconstructed with smoke and mirrors. Trapped: that was my time bomb with a refutable fuse that was lit by the astrological arsonist from the irregular galaxy; that was the premise of my own suspect origin—explosive, but always flowery, yet basic in its entirety.

Ancestrally: that was the derivation of my own personal heritage, for which I could not emphasize more than I could ever understate. Unpolished: that's when I first applied my personal morals with a clear perception of the world as I understood it in the galactic microscope of my personal puerility.

Bluntly: that's when I first came across the remnants of a real human being with an intoxicated spirit. At first, I was confused by the foamy texture of his saga, as well as the folklore of his drunken lore. Not knowing whether I was meeting him at the beginning of a brand-new life or at the end of an inoperative brio (vigor, as well as his own personal vivacity).

All I knew is that he was carrying a bag of rattling bones, changing the fortunes of eloquence and ineloquence, in perpetuum.

Long-winded, blathering, never-ending: that was the best way to describe him, as well as the provenience of a chattering, flighty, light-headed declaimer. One day, he would go on to exclaim that he was the ineloquent drunkard of The Prismatic Glen, who dreamed about his own personal, eloquent souvenirs, titles, even hoity-toity, as well as sober coronations, likened to the futility of a sotted, irresponsible mutilation; from the nature of his own body, and the spirit of his own sorrow.

Discontent (the very next day): *Nurturing, storing, and even preserving; that's when we both interred the skeletal remains of The Euphemist, The Godfather of Infantile Ghosts by The Twin River of Echoes, akin to The Lore of Introspection* (speaking of myself, that's exactly what I was), and then he left, going about his own personal business, preparing for battle; with, and among the wakes of vultures that were also feeding at a carcass.

Generously: that was just one of the many titles I accepted; divinely, but gratuitously, and always affectionately, from the applications of the metaphysical life-forms, and the applications of the earthly trials that I will have to experience in my lifetime; where we will all share something in common.

Coincidentally, that's when I first came across a hot spring from the terrene of Mother Nature; spewing more columns of boiling water into the objectified atmosphere. Gushing, steaming, but not blushing at regular intervals from the curious nature of euphemisms.

Astonished: those were the geysers, and that was the sanity of my own palatial insanity. Social or antisocial, that was my reality, when I was still sane (somewhat), *bright, shining, glittering, chitchatting, yearning for the dark organic matter of my own personal self-discovery.*

Self-applied: I used my own personal techniques, as well as my own personal talents to create, transfer, and then relate the story of my story onto the painter's canvass. That's when the illusion of a real human being toppled, and I was frightened by the articles of my own personal denunciation, as well as the articles of my own personal exculpation; heart-wrenching.

Crystalline: I was unsullied, without distress, and without worry. Longed or unlonged, those were the days of yore; when I was first intertwined with a decorative interpretation of the ever-changing topography.

Key: when the earth was still in dire need of the most proactive, receptive compost. To help express, ensure, and expand the orthodoxy of the most bland composition (as it pertained to the decomposition of vegetable and animal matter, essential to the earth's fertility, as well as its viability).

Gabbling: *Just as much as the excreta, that was the ever-changing pictorial of myself, as well as the earth; with a mythos, as well as a superstitious ambiance. Illustrative, but still composed, by, through, and with a solid coloring matter.*

Vilified or heroically: I was ornamented, infected with an uncensored dialogue that contained ten years of suggestiveness.

Hereof: *Sensually: I was balmy, marked with rays of light that were intercepted by the lampshades of comparative darkness, leaving me jabbering, with the prospect of an undignified hereafter. Upset, that was the indication of my personal vitriol, highly caustic, severe in its effects. That's because I still didn't have a name, all I had was a sobriquet that left me depressed, and want to start crying next to the word autonomy, by the cold and bitter feeling of loneliness.*

Chapter 2

Enter: The Philosophical State of More Bizarre Monographs

Following the musical direction of life, where the musical notes, and the same musical chords were also the same, smallest morphemes. Bowdlerized by the same grammatical pundits, as well as the same embellishing wordsmiths that ran out of words, and had to make up their own.

All of this and all of that was also synchronized by the hour hands of they, them, us, and even we. But what if, or of course, they were also connected to the same minute hands of time, and of course, they were also connected to the same hour hands of ancient civilizations, with a much broader, and a much more expansive vocabulary than the current civilization on planet earth could ever comprehend.

Standing upright by the flagpole: tugging on the heartstrings of the universal definitions, raising the flags of universal sovereignty. Waving hello and goodbye in the hymns of the wind. All of which were expelled, censored, or even condemned by the same universal dictionaries. Somewhere beyond the clouds, with an infinite ladder that I could not seem to ever climb alone without being afraid for my life.

Concerning this and explaining that, furthermore, they were also the same firebrands of literature that were encompassing my inner worldly exceptions. Bounteous, applying their own personal usage of words. Differently, but still imprecise, redundant and always rogatory (as it pertained to asking and requesting), *not necessarily useless, or just unneeded.*

Precisely, I could feel the buzzing in the air, braiding, and upgrading interlocution. I could feel the allure of the earthly, winsome sounds, from the otherworldly messages that were also trying to communicate; by, through, and with me; including the countless insects of the world.

De trop, that was my prophecy, usefully or essentially. I could smell it in the wisdom of the nitrogen: exuberant, qualifying my own lungs, inhaling and stimulating my own visions, but not profuse or unnecessarily.

As of now, that was my skinny body of knowledge, infant; insofar as emaciated, for the purpose of my own personal imagery and the purpose of my own personal visual effects to the point of sesquipedalian. That was the diction of my sensationalism.

Discursive, I was digressive, rambling through the intolerable crevasses of the earth's valleys, where I first found a temple of inquisitive archaeologists that would help me unbury the lifeless history of Mother Nature, as well as the future of my own introspection.

Preposterous, but that was my passion, as well as every other type of life-form that ever wondered about their own fibers and gene pools. With their own personal constitutions, helping me define it, for myself, as well as the observers of the earth's designation.

Amassing: those were the ringleaders of my own impending tour. Festering with blisters and an overload of skin rash. Itching, scratching, making me more uncomfortable in my own skin, as well as my own home, not to mention my own flowerbed of opinions. But those were the knaves of the unrealized encounters, irritating my own personal hankering.

Those were the meddlers, as well as the lousy agitators that could, would, and should incite the rabble-rousers of the bountiful world, crawling on me with an extensive number of issues, problems, as well as bugs, and alien influences, incessantly.

Questionably, that was my paranoia, outlined with a special mechanism: a timepiece designed for the highest accuracy, adjusting the length of my life with a transcendental emission of right and wrong.

Sufficiently, with a consecrated dichotomy, that was exported from the avant-garde of obsolete introspection; interpolated with a vague, distinctive pattern of imagery, as well as a vague, distinctive pattern of indirect expressions.

That would be my lexicon, bristling, quilled, but always exciting, and always superlative, thronged with a chock-full of metaphors and unequalled extravagance with a stark extravaganza.

Purely or impurely, the world will end, and so will the flight of the pinions. One day, for everyone, but if not for everyone, then surely it will for me. Yet I was disciplined, still principled by the utmost changes, when I was still encircled by the rolling hillsides of the earth's applause.

Successfully, I was able to escape the leeward side of reality. However, I was ever frightful of the revolving asteroids that were aiming for planet earth from the depths of outer space and could potentially end the curious nature of human taxonomy.

Terminable: that was my epoch, fascinating, yet it was also the period of the guardians. Answerable or unaccountable, they were the mammals, and they were the safe keepers. They were the primates, and they were the acculturation of sentinels, entrusted to protect, advance, and edify the earthly gardens of God, also known as the human race, with or without condition.

Chiefly, I began to grow with a rhythmic beat that was only found in misconfigured minds, as well as an interlaced pigmentation of my own resemblance to the bastions of unalloyed morbidity, as well as the bastions of disdainful mortality. Vanished: those were the beacons of my childhood, as well as the beatitude of my nervy authenticity.

Exalted: when I was old enough I finally started painting an original portrait of a reproductive floret in the sunrise of my embryonic rant. Malnourished, that's when I mistook the air for a bowl of cereal, and the rain for a glass of milk, and the definitions of my own words for the silverware that I called, the forks and spoons of my introspective lore.

Decapitating the animosity of the scorpions by noon, incapacitated by all of my love, as well as all of my adoration for their existence, near and dear to my heart, as well as my thoughts.

Oh dear, oh dear, I was confabulating with the napkins that we all used to wipe away the breadcrumbs from our mouths. At dinnertime, exemplifying bad manners, poor eyesight, as well as bad instincts. That's when I assumed an alias and rewrote the book of etiquette, as well as the book of biological sciences under the allonym Otherworldly Trope.

Blemished or unblemished: I was in the process of a grandiloquent change and transformation. Ethereally, I was adulterated, but those were the examples of my own metaphorical pleasures. And those were the displeasures as the exhibitionist of the inchoate morbidity, where I exuded more confidence in life. Moderating, and then alleviating the temperaments of the most important predators the earth has ever threatened me with, when I could not lead by example, or follow my own advice.

Spoofed: I was scoffed, but that's where I thrived under the impression of the horrific immortality. Even so, that's where I excelled and was nearly euthanized for it. Flushed down the drain, self-monitoring—I guess that's what I deserved and would likely be penalized for it again, in more ways than I could ever imagine.

Squeezed, mangled, suffocated, nearly crippled to death by the backstairs of hell that cut off the natter of my own anatomy with slivers of wood from the bark of metaphorical trees. As time went on, I was pulled out of the ground by the same little boy from The State of Concupiscent, Euphotic Benevolence, giving me away to the same little girl that he would love until they both died, separately, but in correspondence, as well as a direct correlation to The Twin River of Echoes: two visionaries that were bonded together, born and buried from The Original State of Euphoric Diaries and Personal Memoirs.

Someway, somehow; in one form or the other, *we were all classified, tied together. Endearingly, she was the same little girl that also held me gently, placing me in a glass vase on a windowsill that was half full of water.* Inactive: *that's where I became dull, but more self-observing, sluggish, even lazy: fruitless but still self-examining.*

Twiddling: that was my figurative language, as well as my figurative fore fingers. That's where I sat for more than a year and a half com-

municating with the prating worms, as well as the hordes of centipedes, soaking in the sun with an augury of linguistics that would help attune and harmonize me with an extrinsic future.

Windows: they were my vitreous view to the world. Zooming in: that was the great stampede when society was overrun by mobs and destructive hellions. As a counterpoint, or so it was said, either way, until it was discovered that they were less-fortunate people than I ever was: politically incorrect, socially awkward, obviously rejected by the standards of society, just as I was. If not I will be, durably. Disgracefully, they were the gangs of euthanasia, indecent, but always self-righteous.

That Was The Punishment

Some of which were dismembered by the unearthly creativity of euphemisms, beheaded in the numinous gallows for the crimes that were litigated, prosecuted, and consequently convicted.

Agreeably or unarguably, guilty or not guilty. Questionably, they were sentenced by a jury panel of ignoramus, blatant subservience, prompting the great quote: "Do unto others, but do not do unto others, unless you would like for them to do unto you, exactly the same, as you have done upon them."

Perspicacious: *those were the judgmental hominoids of anthropology* (said of the biological superfamily *Hominoidea*), *judging other people before looking at their own pattern of servility, with an overabundance of conforming duteousness, primarily for the color of their beliefs, which I never fully understood, until I was old enough to decipher the meanings, and the usage of their own bureaucratic terminology.*

Enclosed by the subconscious intonation of life, not only in my premonition, but in retrospect as well, sacrificing the authenticity of my own life in exchange for the process of the earth's evolution—contemporaneously.

Thinkable: that was the unwritten agreement, offensive, and somewhat unwelcome between the unlawfulness of life and the lawfulness of commonsensicality.

Unbelievably, those were the first atrocities that were committed by mankind, affecting the bounteous beatitude of the solemn flowerbeds when I was too small, and I was too immature to do anything about it.

Systematically, I was monotone. Annoyingly, I was even insignificant to the world's social structure, but not to the receptive arms of the universe as a runaway child from the depths of outer space that lost himself in the epoch of his own conformability, as well as the future of monitored time.

Desisted, I was forborne, but still flourishing with a scrap and a scar of my own potential. Contradictorily, only my sagacity and percipience was actually factual in the newborn age of my uncertainty when I was still blossoming with fictitious shades of prominence, as well as nonfictitious shades of interpersonal doubt.

Contestably, the time bomb went off. Upshot: I was erected into the atmosphere, enthusiastically with an inner envelope of my own floral leaves, baptized, and integrated with a plentitude of appreciation and thoughtfulness, just as much as a conjunction of sovereignty.

With regards to the clod and sod, that was my kindness. Giving, that was my gift to the elements of Mother Nature, whom I loved and loved me in return. I just wouldn't know it until my last day on earth.

Lovingly, that was the feministic theory of a woman's nurture and nourishment, her concepts. Said of charades, those were the qualities of the grand terrain that gave us all life. For that, I would gladly acquiesce, on a whim, or a simple request. Accountable, that was the ownership that I took as a personal tribute to the earth, cast forth with a contemptible spell.

I was gushing from the ears, just like the wellsprings of Mother Nature. Steaming, reidentifying myself with the earth's surface, habitation, even its greatest appellations.

Rough and coarse: that's when I was sucked out from the window seal by the specialized winds of change, fitfully, with a medicinal potion of my own disgust and anger, having to adapt to the duologues, as well as the unmeasured temperaments of the quadrate morbidity.

Recurring: episodically, at first, but then I became more and more pleasant, enjoyable, even amicable—eventually becoming more domes-

ticated before reverting back to the wild state of a feral, undomesticated life-form.

Anticipating instability, I was constantly fluctuating from my original state of blissfulness, emitting fragrances from the guild of my own botanical lineage, stemming from the cusp of my exotic corolla, passionately, aurally, and ingenuously.

Speaking abstractly but genuinely and vehemently, I was biologically affected by the environment, so much that my fettered spirit was unchained from the concrete landing space of my own introspection.

Clank, Clank

Remorselessly, turning the pages of my own dissemblance to and from the chapters of my own life, from the infancy of the indicated crib; to the honeybees that I befriended in my quest for sovereignty.

Buzz, buzz—they were my newest friends in life. Buzz, buzz—they were The Pollinators. Buzz, buzz—they were the swarms of bees. Buzz, buzz so that I could basically begin to reproduce. Someday, collecting nectar from the surfeit of my stamens, sticking to the hairs of their delicate, brittle bodies.

Buzzing ardently from sunrise until sundown. They were always furnishing honey to the local merchants. A few in exchange for their yellow jackets, which I thought was a fair trade, and I assumed to honor them, as well as protect them from the rain, as well as the simulation of their slighting omnishambles. Or so it was said that they once had a greater purpose in life, for which I could not prohibit from flavoring the savory tastes of my own selection.

Palatable, those were the prominent choices of the earth's rose petals—delectable, yet combining them with an array of herbs and spices to make herbal tea for the elderly folk, waiting to die in the graced halls and walls of retirement homes.

Accrued: the bees were the ones that helped fertilize me when I was young and little, as well as my beliefs, giving birth to the presentiment of the flapdoodle ordeal. Foretelling, that's when I felt inferior to the massive trees, as well as the massive nomenclatures; built by the spirit, as well as *the galvanization of the earth's first and last invigoration, fertilized by the ashes of my own creation, as well as the dust particles of the earth's divinity.*

Naively, I expected they would one day help guide me toward the passageways of my own self-possession, for which I had no other guiding light to lead me into the perpetual vaults of the sloping absolution or show me the way to the refuge of a more mutualistic relationship with Mother Nature so that I could eventually live the best life that I could possibly live, under the canopy of her umbrella.

Giving in, Succumbing

Submitting to the trope, periodically, as well as the wisdom, and the customs. Bowing, I curtsied to the sounds of the tribal echoes that resounded in the prairies. Edifyingly, I was kneeling, wondering, thinking out loud; when I first felt inclined to bow to the flowers of the consumptive meadows; as an extension of my own personal courtesy and as a respectful sentinel of the earth.

Recommencing: The Story of My Life with an Enchanting Intonation, as Well as the Spiritual Tenet

Mind-bending: that's when I first began to delve, intently, further and further into the art of self-introspection, and I was nearly disposed of for it. So I replanted myself, and I began rising; again, for the second time, from the black holes of my own bottomless prisms. Authentically and individually from the history of the sounds and soil; vigorously, strenuously, and laboriously; day after day, year after year, even after being buried in the earth's regiment of its own sediment for the longest period of time.

Labored and besmirched: I was spoiled by the viands of Mother Nature. Repeating myself, hardened by the overuse of such extravagance, but those were the superlatives of my own locution, as well as the embellishments of my youth.

Satirically, I was newly fertilized with verbalism, intermingling with the stench ordure. Characteristically, through the lineage of my own silt and flavor; which consisted of salt and pepper, as well as a dash of my own inseparable splendor.

KABLOOEY: *prodigal, prodigal—that was my nightmare, the one that I could not detach myself from or ever amend. Indentured, but then it all went away; depreciative, but it was still permissible, inconsiderate, even thoughtless and shortsighted.*

Negligent, said of my feelings and of my personal ennoblement. Enlarged, I was apotheosized, briefly, but then I was shot up into the air by the actions of divine intervention, ejecting me into the era of uncommon extremities, dramatic, but still diverse, and always making me worldlier from life's experiences, occupied by the spectacular creatures of Mother Nature.

Lauded, I was elevated. Yet I still had to share my home with the rodents, and I still had to coexist with the inhabitants of The Prismatic Glen, as expressed in the subliminal story of my own self-portrait. I called it self-absorbed, The Lore of Life's Lessons, self-healing, somewhat therapeutic.

Obscene and grossly indecent: I returned to the woods and began digging for an heirloom of my own creation. Anatomically; I could not find the placenta, in myself, or in the ferns, as well as the related plants, the part of the ovary that bore the ovules; the same tissue that gave rise to the sporangia, problematical to my biological senses.

Knowingly, I was comprised of debasement; innately extrinsic; but those were the peculiarities of the dead leaves. In this case they resembled a mixture of decaying, organic substances, as well as a mixture of efflorescent analogies that were feeding off of my introspective body of knowledge.

Cultivated by the love for my botanical heritage, dealing with matters of psychology, as well as the fabric of my sentimentality. I was fecundated with more piles of rancor, tremendously, as well as more piles of defiance that were commonly associated with overzealous societies.

Forgive me, forgive me not, for the color of my skin, as well as the color of my family portrait. Those were my core values; in life as well as death.

Put on a pedestal: that was my expansive vocabulary, aggrandized, consisting of soliloquies, as well as exenterating monologues. Unreproached, eviscerated from the bowels, as well as the intestines; unsettling, discharging dregs of artless excrement into the ecosystem, as well as the good of the candid jargon that didn't have any kind of restrictions on it; embedded deeply into the genetics of my own histrionic soul; sewn and threaded with fibrous material that was beautified, gnarled, but always contorted, and always twisted by the same filaments of the forthcoming arachnids.

Cunning, cagey, interconnected: that was the parlance from the prophetic nature of spiders that liked to weave their webs and crawl on me with their fuzzy, bristly hairs, tickling my nostrils, making me chortle with a superficial likeness to the gleeful chuckles of the uncustomary frontispiece.

Giving me an option for more allegorical speech, making me diverse, from here to my past, and from my past to my own eventuation; about information, as well as knowledge, as it pertained to the worldly and otherworldly features of the world, even the universe that nourished our values from afar; with honorable mention, as well as an honorable membership; where I carved my own niche in the antechambers of the world's morbidity.

Faced and defaced, I was tortured; by, through, and with the micturition of life, as well as the micturition of the cloud's downheartedness (as it pertained to the raindrops of the chagrined, dispirited conservation).

Circumlocutory as a roundabout expression. I was drowning, but then I was revived to life by the dignity of an idealized Deity. That's when I first worshipped the earth's bionomics, and all of its beautiful rose petals.

Unsurpassable: those were the colors of undeniable ecstasy. Figuratively, my introspection was uncultivated, but still regimented; by, through, and with every blade of grass; rented; by, through, and with every vibe of communication.

Quelled by the dandelions that tried to laden me, and over-tower me, even outshine me, I called it self-preservation, when it was really just selfishness, if not jealousy, and I should've been much more receptive than

I really was, and I apologize for that. From being buried in the earth's proliferation for millions and millions of years. I guess that was my family history, I guess that was my imperfection.

Periphrastic (in a much more roundabout way), *or unpretentious; in a more subtle, but direct expression, that's what I called hypocrisy, but still looking for an original name. With or without a face; I was accentuated by the double standards of the ligaments, and the lamented human beings, none of which I could reclaim, or especially discard. Not today, and not tomorrow; but maybe one day, when I turn the last page of my own life that is measured by the wispy calendars of time.*

Claimed or unclaimed, plowed or unharrowed, upturned or rototilled; emotionally and intensely, those were the thorns of my self-observation. Plotting, burning; realizable, those were the thorns of my prickliness, disguised as an inherent quality of the pinnate-leaved shrubbery that was commonly associated with illustrated parables.

Detonated: I reexploded upon the scene. This time I was more serviceable, businesslike, starry-eyed, bursting forth with a measurable level of zest; billowing under the firestorm of equality.

Surprisingly, I was even more combustible, and yet I was much more feasible, smoldering with plumes of smoke (a mixture of heat particles and gases), *when we were all capable of being killed: by, through, and with the effects of smoke inhalation.*

Contradicted by the great floods of inequality, dowsing me with their floral ribbons of universal pageantries, as well as fire retardant from the ivory-towers of their inner-worldly scorchings. That's when we were all capable of drowning with a measurable level of malfeasance.

Abrasive: that was the antithesis, *causing more idealism and friction in the universe, between myself, as well as the earth, chronicled by the emperors of my own nobility, when I first embarked upon the independent journey of a lifetime, without a feminine companion or a glimmering hope that would help put me in a meditative state of solitude.*

Unexpectedly, that's where I first found the opportunity for self-improvement, challenging myself with the opportunity for self-growth, uncovering the treasures of self-worth; somewhere beyond the shrines of a more tender, compassionate prophesy.

Speaking Anonymously

Quite frankly, I am what I am, if you cannot accept me for who or what I am, then please exclude me from your own personal journey so that I may be able pursue my own personal, extravagant dreams; with or without condition, in the harbor, or the mud puddles of the earth's preservation. This is my life; meshed or unmeshed, with or without pre-conceived notions.

Metamorphosis: conceptualizing the inception of the redeco-rated realism with an effeminate characterization of the most gor-geous roses, stems, even the most gorgeous rose petals that were insufferably displayed by their outlines.

Exactly, I was incarnate, fleshly, elated. Said of spirit, mind, and body, provided with an ultimatum. Delicately, I was everything that a prospective man in life could ever want out of his own imagery. Softly, I was nothing that a prospective man in life could ever want out of his own exaggeration in the same span of time.

Of whom, what, when, or why: symbolic, elucidating the funda-mental laws of my grammatical slurs. As expressed, those were the myth-ical aisles of my serenity; the same ones that no other man or woman could ever begin to comprehend, intensifying the caldrons of my domicile. Henceforth, altering the acrimonious roads of my fate forever.

Delineated through the lens of an anecdotal cathedral: *Bounded by the essential features of cultivation. I was born as the embryo of self-in-trospection, with or without a name, but only a by-name and denomina-tion. Yet I was always blessed with the pedigree of a misguided aspirant into the elongated domain of the incisive, spherical globe, where anything and everything in life could occur, prevail; even dominate the outlook of my vivaciousness.*

Clear and direct, I was enticed. Cut, recut, and then I was lured, unbounded by the grandeur pastures of prosperity, in the same year of uncertainty; when I was rebounding, and could no longer tell the differ-ence between the enemy of the rosebush, and the friends of the analytical shrubbery; except for a few pesky, anatomically incorrect figurines, mak-ing it blurred, and somewhat indistinct.

Repressed, that's where I first met Gadfly, The Lore of Extrospection (part man, part warble fly). *Yodeling: trilling, warbling on the outskirts of the earth's botanical gardens. Caroling, his morbid songs of sovereignty, that were also blowing out my eardrums, as well as anything, and everything that has ever been beautiful about the arty, ornate realm of Mother Nature, leaving me deaf for nearly twelve consecutive months. Faultlessly, that was one full year before I was able to get a new set of eardrums.*

Unearthed: he was a mutant after all. Ephemeral, he was also fugacious, a.k.a. Rococo, The Volatile Extrovert of The Prairies, accentuating himself from the ancient times of unperturbed flamboyancy.

Needling, he liked to prick me, bite me, annoy me, as well as the rest of the earth's domestic animals. Yet he also provoked other people, with his criticism, and with his schemes; with his nonfunctional ideas, and with his outrageous demands, dirtied by the unfeasible requests of impracticality. Useless, he was becoming more of a problem to the body of introspective lore, which was already disfigured by the lamenting sounds of The Twin River of Echoes.

The transformation: speaking from the perspective of the third person, with a jumbled mess of unfeasible trepidation.

Bemused, from the arrows of the archers, and the ivory keys of the targeted pianists that wrote, spoke, and sang songs about them. From the beginning, I was the variant of life, uninhibited by the consternation of my own physiognomy, so I was transformed into an iconic figure of introspection, making me much more influential to the world, as well as its famed annals.

Oddly, a few years later, I met a gaudily, vulgar four-hundred-year old pirate by The Twin River of Echoes. The very next day. I was mortified and bought a brand-new bicycle from The Magnifico Merchant of Costumes. Sequentially, I wanted to ride it, all the way to the pearly gates of heaven; beyond the clouds and beyond my own conclusion of time and space.

Poof—magically, that's when the bicycle became a lifelong acquaintance and we were both predisposed. Useful and much more operable to the world as a whole, and we were both set astir. Then I began to petal my way through the dirt trails of the burlesque omens. Said of birthright, as well as the birthplace of sovereign expeditions. That was the emana-

tion of my own personal temptation, always hovering, somewhere in the uncelebrated compartment of my own conscientious brain.

More precisely, that was the translucent edifice, where I first resided as an introspective option of the earth, mostly and repeatedly, but always dependably. In the mornings, I was more blissful than ever before, with a short sample size of my own morbid history. Modernized, I was imbued by the inspirational feelings of certainty, as well as the inspirational quotes and opinions of my own mythology, but not so much the opinions of others.

Unerringly, I could not foresee the moisture of the colors that were demonizing the bloodlines of my inner spirit, blackening the molecules of my own formidable reputation, abundantly as well as the colors of my impeccability. Once, they were the color of my seeds. Now, they were the color of my conspicuous projection, airy, red.

Reserved or unreserved, that was my liveliness, as well as my remembrance of when I was just a little organism; in reference to the true blue dot of outer space. That was the earth levitating in the darkness of real-located universes. Designed, built, and manufactured, developed with a small amount of neighbors, rotating around the sun. All the while I was trying to figure out the most difficult riddles of my own personal life, even if it was haphazard or in a careless manner.

Assuredly, those were the archives, written and entombed into the physical inclination of the rugged mountainsides, locked away and stored in the innermost tombs of the world's enormous cordillera (those were the chains of mountains, usually the principal mountain system, or the mountain axis with the largest landmass).

And I was a frolicking as a miniscule emblem of the earth, dumbfounded by the pheromones of the life-providing planet, as well as the nucleus of a self-sustaining star.

Bosh, bosh, more bosh, defining pheromone: the nuance of the nuisance (any chemical substance released by the animal serving to influence the physiological behavior of other members from the same species).

Luckily for me, this time I avoided being trampled by the forces of Mother Nature, throttled, crushed, destroyed by the most grisly wildlife, gargantuan, mammoth in their size, as well as their sorrowful theories.

Regardless, I was still able to savor the memoirs of my own youthful exuberance. Agreeably, that was universally accepted. From the time I was a little boy to the time and place that I would eventually become a transformational, introspective man of the world, a child forever and ever through the eyes of the unharnessed Lord.

Channeling and then harnessing my energy, no matter how old I was. I was always encouraged and supported by my belief and my support in the omnipotent father. Awe-inspired by the creed, as well as my faith, I was tranquilized by the most exquisite dream that an unfettered algorithm of the earth could ever dream about, motivated to pursue the most important things in life that were near and dear to my heart, as well as my head, shoulders, even back, neck, and feet; but especially my psyche, as well as the shock absorbers that would absorb the greatest amount of turbulence. Those were my legs, otherwise known as my metaphorical stems.

Presupposing: those were the hyperboles. Attested or unattested, they were the antecedents, objectionably, just as much as they were my fellow brothers and sisters; collaboratively; stigmatized; by the foundation of the monumental circumstances, as well as the foundation of the monumental, crumbling, stepping stones.

Possible or nonviable, I was initially transgressed by the multitude of generational bridges, but not as much as the gap of generational divides, so I began training, steadfastly with an irresistible compulsion, to reveal the mysteries of the world that were all veiled by the ghoulish history of the great unknown. Tugging, pulling, ripping me apart. Focused, slowly, but surely, methodically putting me back together.

That was the miraculous recovery of life. Healing by The Twin River of Echoes, when I was listening to the headless psychologists, sociologists, and even the fruits of brainless, psychiatric care.

Unswayed: that was the irresistible impulse of the greatest thing that ever complemented the word amalgamation. *I called it self-introspection; others called it metamorphosis. Pressing, hurried, and always in a rush, I was assertive. So much that I called it—"spilling my guts, as well as my blood." For the urgency of the glory, as well as the mantras of tightly clustered divisions that believed in the overall cause. Inspired: that was the basis for my assortment of catchphrases, as well as my assortment of distinctive cries, including my personal virtues.*

Vibratory, I was paranoid, from here to the end of solidity, with a reconfiguration of my own serenity. Those were the things that made me who and what I was—today, tomorrow, and forever. Shaking, trembling, blending my thoughts and emotions into the airy space of the earth's hemisphere, wondering about the origin of life, as well as the taste buds of death; swallowed by, through, and with the smallest portions of pride, as well as acid reflux, even the overtones of my displeasures, laced with rampant saliva. Those were the pleonastic rains of my onerous journey.

That's when I began investigating, encroaching and rummaging through the history of the world with the pace of a lethargic snail. Studious, but that's when I also discovered my own history when I first found the ashes of the world's dead roses.

Swathed or unswathed: that was my own future, packaged, bandaged, enfolded; enveloped, by, through, and with the prettiest ribbons, wrapped around my body, someday sealing my fate.

Jaw-dropping: those were the dead leaves that have come before me, and I was determined to reinstall their spirits; reinvigorate them while standing on the fringe of the existential landscape that had oxygen and hydrogen all around it; breathable, but still recognizable from the perspective of heaven.

Surely, that was my connection to the liminal line of demarcation, mythologized with an attractive description. Wisp, wisp, sprawling with a remnant and a slender trace of my own personal speculation, as well as a slender trace of microbes that helped reproduce more oxygen with mysterious degrees of unimaginable consequences, making me more jittery than ever before with a tremulous sensation. That was the characterization of my own nervousness, when I was metamorphosed into an introspective man; willfully or unwillfully.

Chapter 3

Voyager, the World Traveler

S *tirred, whisked, and aroused: I woke up next to the poetically rhyming words of the ever-transcending sunlight, traveling into the beloved housing that was built on the framework of diffusing introspection; with slabs of concrete that were forming the Paladins of the most uncomplimentary palaces.*

Tragically, as a guest, or as a stranger, I was roving about, without an escort or a friendly face to call a friend; ambulating, traipsing, aimlessly, from the abstruse cellars of my own hellholes, to the more practical attics of reality that had a higher grade about them.

Beset: that was the presentiment; presenting me with the most otherworldly opportunities that blackened the lightest side of the moon, but only by, through, and with my own perceptions of morbidity.

Ethically or unethically, that's where I began to search for the curtains of the world's history, as well as the juncture of the world's future; behind the scenes, and behind the universal stage of such critically acclaimed performances.

Outcast: that's where I began circling, rolling, tumbling about, with the wheels of life, and the curtains of the world's galactic pits, even the curtains to my own living rooms; estranging myself, from the earth itself so that I could one day hide my view of unsolidified assurance; and then blame it on my own riled dizziness.

Confirmed: that was the degree of importance, the one that I was looking for; from the day I was born, to the day I will die, and could never seem to find, underneath a rock, or a musty carpet place.

Regathering myself: I started looking everywhere else in the universe, even the definitions of asteroids, as well as their doomsday appellations. Insinuating delirium prose, including the past, just as much as the future, except for the only place that I should've looked for in the first place, but I never did, until it was too late. That was many years ago, when I look back on my life, many years in the future.

If I had to do it all over again, I would go back there and never leave in the first place. Changing the definition of introspection, as well as the course of human events that took place by the flames of the old wives tales; dowsed and discredited, unlimited; dying with the same annuals that were submerged by The Twin River of Echoes.

That was the holy edifice, that was my church, and that was my bible, turned into the same heartbeat of my own faith, as well as the same heartbeat of my own journey for sovereignty. That was my mistake, the one I neglected, providing me with a greater purpose in life, to correct the things I could still change, but regret the things in life that I could not change; forcing me to go through the journey of life alone, even if it does cost me my life. Before any of this or any of that will ever happen again, occur, or ever transpire.

Enchanted or disenchanted: that was the never-ending quest, for myself, as well as The Sovereign Timekeepers of The Escalators to Heaven. Those were the loftiest expectations, for the national anthem, and the homage of the nations that was sung by the voices of the bees, suppressed by the voices of their own honorable morbidity. About me, as well as them, about all of us: unified, morbidly, with or without statuesque stability.

Presumptuously, when I returned to the earth, I could not determine who and what the demons really were, vandalizing my own personalized ambitions; tinted with an aura from the entrance points of the bewailing abyss, as well as the memories of the profound euphoria; darkly, from the exit points of my own disinterest.

Thoughtfully morbid; reasonably, but still irrational, and always in denial.

Insistent, I don't think I am obsessed with death. I just think about it a lot. Accumulative, those were the sculptors of my own personal brain, as well as the ingredients that helped nourish my bloodstream.

Still in Denial

Overly concerned: I was retransitioned by the ingredients that helped nourish my vital organs, reluctantly. Every day thereafter, I thought about acceptance, as well as the repercussions of my own personal morbidity.

Disqualifying myself; that was the infatuation of the soul that I could not be freed from or ever absolved. Unless I died, which might be the best thing for everyone involved.

Buzzing, fuzzing, rushing in the background of the morbid cussing.

Those were the supplications of my own vitality, as well as the prospects of my own lifelessness that befuddled me. Understandably or defiantly, I tried to collect the minerals from the deadliest river in the history of eloquence and sovereignty, with an otherworldly endeavor, trying to cross the liminal line of demarcation, redirecting the asteroids of outer space. For the evolution of my self-evolution and the evolution of another dimension, but I was advised with caution by the constancy of unrestricted extremities.

Boo

Those were the ghosts and those were the great philosophers that offered me advice on how to kill myself and still be accepted into heaven, if that was even possible. I called it—optimizing, the unfeeling and underlying aspect of my own morbidity. Others called it suicide; I preferred to call it—optimistically challenged as a secondary option. Extreme, extreme, but giving me notice—legitimately, as well as subcon-

sciously, when I first thought that I couldn't distinguish the quirks or the affectations of my newest friends and foes.

Served with a gentle warning of reproof, as well as a gentle warning of forbearance.

Rivaled, I was bespattered, attempting to sever my ties with the most reprobate, intimidating shadows that were also following me; to and from the false footing of The Twin River of Echoes.

(Buzz, buzz)

They were always stalking me. At first, I thought they were the bees, but then I couldn't tell the difference between the bees and the devil's work. Yet I could still hear the noises in the background that were always ringing in my ears.

Pushing the boundaries of what was possible and what was not by the candlestick of the ancient demon that disguised himself as the most lovable caricature in my odyssey for sovereignty. Burning at a thousand degrees Celsius, I just couldn't tell who, what, when, or where he was; unless he presented himself to me as the face of Satan.

(Buzz, buzz)

Threatening me, making me believe that I was going to be eaten alive, as a coal of the earth or a friend of the flowers that used my morbidity as his own personal supply of unlimited oxygen.

Buzzing, buzzing, buzzing.

Seldom did I ever think that I was actually going to be eaten alive (buzz, buzz), *but I was timid of the shadows, as well as the demons, and because of that I was also fearful, not because of their presence, but because of the unknown, and what they might represent—my hellish destiny.*

(Buzz, buzz)

That was a flash.

(Buzz, buzz)

That was a look into the end of my life as I had never known it before.

(Buzz, buzz)

Nor would I ever victimize or wish it upon anyone else that was already comforted by the scriptures of their own peace and tranquility.

For which I could only wish that I had myself. That's what I called categorical jealousy.

Humming—large, ample, copious, even spacious, exhibiting traits of fullness that only yielded to traits of emptiness.

Plentifully: those were my words. Inwardly; they were also my thoughts, just as much as I was wary of them. More defensive; externally, I was constantly looking up and down, all around me; waiting to be burned alive, or waiting to be uplifted from the earth itself. That was called salvation, and I was always watchful of the unexplored territory.

Immersing myself more deeply, prefaced by the endorsements of my heart-whole intentions; outwardly, as it pertained to my own personal euphemisms. I was mindful of my latest surroundings, but only partially attentive to the most intricate details and designs of my newest profile.

I am much more formidable after all, physically imposing, with my own stature, as well as my own memories of flowerbeds, even my own proposals that made me thicker than thin, half-heartedly, narrow and long. Full-heartedly, lanky and wise, but always unwisely careless; sincerely, but most definitely thoughtful, and always striving to be the best person that I could possibly be.

Commonsensible, I asked the bees and the ghosts to join me in the wee hours of my admonishing adventure. That was the morning of optimism and overwhelming reflection, when I could not be burned alive or caressed by the flames of fire that crackled with the midnight charcoal. Snapping, crackling, popping, rubbing my shoulders with the residue of the burning wood that created more carbon monoxide, but gave me warmth, life, peace of mind, just as much as the possibility of a deathly epithet.

All of this was done so that I could not be alone, and so that I would not be circumvented by the wind flurries of Mother Nature's whistling, as well as the wind funnels of her choirs and my own emphatic circumference. Taking caution so that I would not be hurried by the mystified guise of my own impatience.

Yet their leader rejected me. The term Gadfly came to mind; unceasingly.

(Buzz, buzz)

Peacefully, with or without commotion and hostility.

(Buzz, buzz)

Swearing up and down that they would never go away; even in my darkest hours.

(Buzz, buzz)

When I least expected it, or when I most expected it.

(Buzz, buzz)

That was the great mystery that I could not seem to disentangle. Considerately, indicating the choice was never mine and they were always going to be with me for the rest of my life; whether I liked it or not.

(Buzz, buzz)

Snared, I was caught in their trap. A human being entangled by the webs of spiders (bunched in clusters and clutters), *forcing me to read out loud, about the most repugnant critters in the world. In accordance, as a conformist or a nonconformist, I deferred to their wishes, as well as their wisdom.*

So I spent the next twenty-four hours cohabitating with the bears, as well as the antlers of the hunted deer that were decomposing from the game hunters that killed them for sport, as well as the beavers that were gnawing on the tree bark, building their own dams, but still rooting for the laurels of my own personal elucidation, but only as it pertained to the worldliness of Mother Nature, still ignoring my own personal dilemma of being caught in a trap. I continued to read in subservience.

Through, by, and with my own personal faith, I was disentangled by the spirits of the ladybugs, and the spirits of the inferences that were also guarding against danger, outlining my own personal strategies in life, as well as my own personal strategies in death. That was the day I nearly died of starvation due to a lack of personal knowledge, the worst kind of way for any worldly man to have to die, until I intercommunicated with the multilingual leader of the bees.

And he said to me, in the fairest voice, of all the fairest voices, with the fairest feelings of empathy. Bonsoir, my flowery friend, I love you just as much as I love the fairness of tomorrow, and tomorrow will be a much fairer day—for you, as well as me; for them, as well as all of us.

Then he gave me a spoonful of honey with a cup of tea. At first I thought he was trying to trick me, even poison me (through food and drink), *but I went to sleep instead of dying with the compliance of the ghosts, and the compliance of Mother Nature.*

Staggering, when I woke up, I felt much better. I think he was French or just a drunk little bee with a slur and a proclivity for European dialect. As a tourist, I think he preferred the South American mountain ranges, but only as a regular bee. I think he preferred the shrubs and trees of any old regular forest. Yet that was his lineage. That was his worldliness, as the leader of the bees.

More stupendous: that was the skit that made me studious and more knowledgeable; paying special attention to the other species of the world, not just myself. I liked to call it—the scripture of my own leaves and intellectual awakening.

On the spectacular side of the world, a few weeks later, I met a Russian scorpionfly by the patio decks of the clouds, and he said to me philosophically. Da, da (yes, yes). *Anyway, anyhow. he also had a great fondness for British wineries, German currywurst, even schnitzel, Scandinavian cream, as well as bread, cheese, and even crackers, including oatmeal porridge and mashed potatoes. Of course, he also like pickled cucumber with a side of lingonberries.*

Still searching, not only for my own personal name, but also for the hopes of becoming a worldly man of the world, maybe not today, but tomorrow, and forever there more. Lastingly, I will never stop climbing the stair wells to heaven that will actualize my own handful of dreams.

Confounded: that's when I began scavenging, through the maps of the world and started searching for the encyclopedias, as well as the world almanacs; thinking about the artifacts of the world's history that had yet to be unearthed, as well as the artifacts of my own future that had yet to be lived and lost.

Traveling far and wide, that's where I envisioned a more traditional Chinese festival. When I could not find the answers to my own personal dreams in the postern of my customized hinterland; underneath a rock, or in the copse of other Asian countries, especially underneath the chandeliers of heaven that were also dangling from the universal clouds. They were the sunlit stars of outer space, as well as the planets, and the other debris that threatened our mere existence. But that was the beauty of the celestial chandeliers, pretty; but still deadly in its origin, as well as its natural creation.

Theretofore, all I found was a dictionary with the word Qingming. *Embossed and boldfaced, underlined, but well-defined, especially for me. I think that was my fate. I think it was meant to let me know the minuteness of our own existence; and how relatively small we are by comparison.*

Factually, I wasn't able to decipher the triviality of my own sovereign aspirations (selfish), *before I started the greatest race of a lifetime. That was the race to heaven before hell ever consumed me.*

Yet they were all my dreams, and they were my dreams alone. I think it was to let me know that I was not the center of the universe, because there was a much bigger meaning to the meaning of my life. At least that was my interpretation of the word Qingming, *and that was my own personal experience with a Chinese moth that translated the meaning of the word for me. Tomb-Sweeping Day or Chinese Memorial Day/Ancestors' Day.*

Exhausted, when I came back to the phenomenal side of reality, all I found was an autobiographical heap of indefiniteness, as well as an indefatigable heap of Chinese books and proverbs that spoke mandarin, with immeasurable timetables; elicited from the front pages of my own worldly possibilities.

Proactive—the very next day, I started growing bonsai trees next to the coastlines of Japan after learning about Zen Buddhism, but I failed miserably, as I usually did. Nonetheless, I tried my very best and decided to learn about the springbok. That's when I traveled even farther, and even wider, before returning home, finding myself running alongside the gazelles from the arid plains of South Africa.

Intellectually, I was bloated, and that was my crash course in world zoology, up until this point; and up until tomorrow, when I learn more about the characteristics of the marsupials, from the heartbeat of Australia, to the beauty of the wildlife in the Andes Mountains of South American lore, ranging from Argentina, Bolivia, Chile, Colombia, Ecuador, Peru, and even Venezuela.

Legend had it: those were the archives, said of metaphorical slurs. That was the world vault, stored with bones and ancient relics of vast memories, mostly extinguished values, even architects, planners, designers, as well as adjoining engineers that made up the whole body of architecture. Mummified, but still written by the hand of Mother Nature, scribbled by the doodads of ho-hum, unrealizable humbuggery.

Excluding the torso, blindly, as well as the torqueing joints of elderly men and women. Visibly aged, visibly dying, visibly hungry for a meal from the fountain of youth that even the oldest bugs and fire flies of the world couldn't seem to find, but it still existed, somewhere beyond the campfire stories of the foxholes and fire flies, as well as the ticks and poison oak that were grown and slain; by, through, and with the blades of visualized folklore.

Visually and more colorfully, particularly the aging fellowship was complemented by the lubricated joints of the youngest, renascent flowers. On the agenda, enlarging the lymph nodes that were already impelled by the diaphragms of middle-aged dilemmas.

Scrutinized, physically as well as morally: *measuring me, as well as my glands, the bees helped reconstruct a new home for me. Betide, presenting me with a new title: The Founding Father of Introspective Lore—with more than a quintillion acres that were used for a front lawn.*

Humbly, I could not ask for anything more, not from the bees, except for their companionship, or wish for anything less, giving me the most luxurious accommodations that an introspective dreamer of the world could ever dream about.

By, through, and with the divine counsel of my own creation; that was the eternal flowerbed. Hailed or unhailed; conceptualized, or just not actualized; by, through, and with the flowery pastures of heaven, which I assumed was a much better place to sleep, or just spend time in general.

As a general consensus, it was a much better place to socialize with the culture of the knotty, burly weeds, as well as the culture of their conservative views, comments, or even the confessions of the most time tested cockroaches that have lived through it all.

Fulfilled or unfulfilled, their language was the language that I would study for my own self-preservation. So that I can know the way the world really was, from the beginning of time, and so that I can determine for myself the reason it has become so fundamentally unkempt, subsiding into the apocalyptic black holes of desistance.

Building my foothold.

More liberally, politically inclined or disinclined. I chose to affiliate myself with the pebble stones, and the mulch that were also the friendliest neighbors of morbid minds. Bespoken; fenced or set free; those were the moderate millipedes, without an independent following.

Deeply and emotionally invested, they all watched me build my new home; somewhere in the clouds with dimensional lumber that was milled by the millers, as well as the clod and sod (fertilized soil), *that was foretold by the adumbrations of earthly premonitions.*

Premonished, I wanted to build my new home in heaven, but heaven was too expensive for me at the time. For now, I could only afford the ghettos. As previously asserted, that was The Confines Of No Wheres', right next to The Valley of Everyday Sin.

Admittedly, I was too poor, ragged, unworldly and unworthy of being accepted into heaven; in terms of my own personal morals, morale, or established virtuosity; disqualifying myself from an interview with God; or substantiating the qualities and qualifications of his worthiness.

Inexperienced, I was limited by my own personal youth, lacking life's full experiences, in and amongst the constellations of stars. So that one day I could finally rest in the company of Christ through time-proven spirituality.

In the meantime, my faith was being tested, time and time again, just as my belief was also being tested. On the verge of destruction, that's what I had to look forward too, in order to receive the greatest de facto of eternal liberation.

Prejudiced or unprejudiced, that was the criteria that was presented to me by the flocks of birds, as well as the swarms of bees, when I was still living on planet earth. That was the process of life that I called—life regularly.

Unchanged, in the aboriginal premise of everything, and everyone that has ever aspired to spend eternity; through, by, and with the side of God, sometimes leaving me hungry for more time-honored traditions, as well as time-honored characteristics. In any case, most of which was not applied to me or well-suited for the ill-defined anomalies of an existing, uncoordinated metamorphosis.

Untraditional and very much nonconforming, that's when I became more self-defining; well-spoken but not as well-represented, so I settled for a cheap piece of real estate just below the clouds, but still above the mountainous rooftops of the world's ceilings; such as the Chomolungma (Mount Everest), *goddess mother of the mountains in the Tibetan Plateau, as well as the Huascaran, from the developing country of Peru, or the Chimborazo of Ecuador.*

Towering, alpine, customarily snowcapped; those were the world's highest peaks, when I didn't have a permit to rebuild my home or reside in the grandeur pastures of the afterlife. Interim, that was The Hypothetical Castle in The Sky, partway to heaven and partway to hell.

Grunting, with or without bunting.

Without end and without rest, this was the speech heard around the world. A far cry from The Valley of I Never Sin (for me, that was the loneliest and most remote place on earth), *as told through the view-point of a thousand years of famed, corresponding elm trees. Dismally, as well as the greatest proponents of Mother Nature, dejected, which I affectionately called—the oldest and greatest grandparents of the earth's habitational latticework.*

Arboreal Roots, My Heritage, Said of Gloom and Glum

Choreographed or unchoreographed: that was the great scry (the use of divination to discover hidden knowledge or future events, especially by means of a crystal ball): *repaired, hemmed, and sewn with a Band-Aid from the wool of their national pride, as well as the wool of their national flags, banners, even slogans.*

Symbolic: down below, the bandages fell off of the earth's incisions; posting a bloodied flag, causing a bloodied resonation throughout the world's magnanimous glens.

More centralized: anyone or anything that has ever died in the metaphorical wistfulness of The Twin River of Echoes; one person, one inhabitant, one proper noun; one animal of Mother Nature, for every nation on earth that has ever been liberated or enslaved by the civil or uncivil quilts and patterns of the world's history. Free, but not for long; living, but with an even greater prospect of dying, briskly.

Up above, that's where I continued to grow, and grow, and grow; until my height was compromised by the artistry of the clouds, with more than a thousand words, and more than a thousand years of encouragement, from the smallest and most liberal creatures of the earth that have ever lived and died alongside me.

Interacting: those were the brutes and critters of Mother Nature that have experienced the greatest torments and fires with me. Undivided, we were all banded together; until it all went away from the previous century of neglect and grave dissolution, with an even greater; unmediated pollution.

Prognosticating: that's when I took a glimpse into the future and saw the world as we know it now become unlivable (all because of climate change).

Envisioning, furthermore: that's when I saw the world's polar caps melt away, covering, drowning, immersing the igloos of the Eskimos, and the shorelines of the earth itself, with the innermost topsoil, as well as the forgone topography, like we will never know it again.

Said of killing off the world's polar bears, as well as my roots, including my memories of the animals that used me, or any ordinary tree for their own personal abode; stripping me of my name, depleting me of my energy, as well as my will, including my veins and willingness to change the things that I could no longer change, hopelessly. That's when I lost faith in my caregivers. That was the classification of people known as the human race.

Morose, recurrent, punctually, and ordinarily: that was the great atrocity of the most inept civilization, unwilling to act prudently, but always willing to act hastily. Even so, they were still able to prevent the things that could be prevented.

Winded or unwinded, wonted or unwonted, I still persisted through the windless, mindless diaphragms of the previous century; over-exaggerated, until I was overextended and could no longer breathe. Automatically, my trunk began to break, as well as my spirit, falling apart with the longest branches of indeterminacy that I could not foreswear.

Adjourned: the meeting of the minds was closed for now. Dissociated, suspended, set aside for the next generation of typical, morbid intellectuals, just not the next century of the earth's ruination; deconstructing the infrastructure of the most conceivable trees with a predetermined growth period.

Clear-cutting my namesake, as well as my relatives; incrementally, that would ultimately heighten the effects of climate change. Precipitately; that's when my spirit also died, dissevered and bisected; when we were all capable of destroying the earth; one tree ring at a time.

Joylessly and gloomily: those were the shattered boughs of one thousand year old elm trees, blown away by the components of unpredictability, to smithereens. Disintegrating (as it pertained to the dolefulness of teary-eyed souls).

I will eventually be miscommunicated from the earth altogether. Yet I was born with a bias point of view; and my own heritage will also be melted and vaporized by the ponderous waves of such sublime, as a direct correlation to the children of God that influenced the behavior of the planet in the most self-destructive way imaginable; providing life to the modern homonyms and human beings that helped inflame the temper of the sun's solar flares.

Incommunicado. That's when my feelings were also putrefied, alongside the greatest, combative hours of the earth's introspective lore. Categorically, those were the voices of the old growth forests, and the voices of ancient animals that were censured, but not the voices of the most assertive mountains. Sleeping or active: they will also roar, and then explode until the end of matter, or the earth itself; devastating to the prospect of my own totality, for now, and forever.

Habituated: that was the subliminal message of my own nefarious cruelty; underscored with an overhanging portent. That was my speech, and those were my thoughts. Gallivant, alongside my sentiments, as well as my quizzical predictions.

Sincerely, the decayed, tumbling, oldest and wrinkled rings of The Incommunicative Elm Tree.

Bowing, without a curtain call, or a curtain drop, that was the speech; from a dying breed of elm trees. Faithless: it was still fickle, but free to speak with the history of its own rings that continued to live on.

Once revolved, but no longer revolving, and no longer growing. Spiritually, around the premise, or the premium of life, with or without a semblance of its own euphemisms, allegories, or figurative speech; its heartbeat was stagnant, coy, skittish; depicting the process of metamorphosis as a hefty price to pay; but only as it pertained to climate change.

Chapter 4

Conceptualization

Higher and higher, that was the future, and this was the present. Bigger and bigger, taller and taller, wider and longer: growing luxuriantly. The introspective bicyclist was also becoming more and more lush, stipulating the seconds, minutes, hours, days, weeks, months, and years of his seething chronology. Fulminating and then rediscovering himself with threads of manhood, psychologically, as well as futuristically, just not realistically.

Said of an Appellation (a Name, Title, or Designation: The Act of Naming)

Brazen Maven: that's my name. The one I have been looking for all of my life, just not willing to die for, with, or dreadfully. Even so, I am dumber than God, but still smarter than Satan. It just took me a while to figure it all out. That's because I found a way to differentiate between heaven and hell, somewhere in between. Those were my keynotes, when the voices of the bees began to sing my name, out loud, next to the ivory keys, alongside the violin strings of a ruby red violin.

Buzz, buzz—*those were the meanings of the words, said of courage and expertise. That was my name and what they represented: symptoms, as well as symbols of good and evil. That I was something else, something other than what I originally thought I was.*

Befoul: life was too complex for me, but so were the idioms of my own debauchery, as well as the seriousness of my own morbidity, as well as my mortality, just as much as the idiocies of my own great fallacy.

Bonded: we were all tangled together, uniformly. Externally, we were all divided apart, unpleasantly, simultaneously by the same slandered, mutinous mutineers, as well as the same wickedness of unity.

Still, thinking out loud, simplistically, as well as vociferously. Positively, as long as there is curiosity in the universe there will always be a theatre for unraveling the mysteries of the great unknown.

Exposing, pinching, revealing, those were the stencils, painted with mellifluous metaphors of sinful pride. Ordinary or unaccustomed, trademarking the polka dots of humanistic faults, one speckle at a time.

Connecting the dots to the diagrams that were coded; by, through, and with the same unbreakable bonds: *As long as I am still alive, I will never be able to stop reading, writing, learning, loving, living, cooking, or looking for something else in life that may or may not exist, but matters to me altogether, more than anything, or anyone in the history of the world can ever know.*

Exonerating himself: *As long as I can still breathe I will always be able to disperse and broaden the scope of my ever-expanding horizon. Losing focus: that's when I had to regather myself and concentrate on the road ahead of me, losing sight and feel of the earth's fertility—pillaging, discoloring the organic messages of the earth's terrain, as well as my own applications of death, slaughtering the grapevines of my own personal dreams, assassinating the flyspecks and mites of my sovereign quest.*

Disreputably: those were the dials, as well as the solar flares that would make it all happen. Peacefully or aggressively, when I was comforted by the blankets, knitted by one hundred year old ladies in wooden rocking chairs, weaving the fibers of my own personal resilience, with the fibers of my own personal resolution; the very same ones that would likely kill me, without a second thought.

Nonchalant: that's when I had no one to comfort me by the floral beauty of The Twin River of Echoes. The bees were busy with summer, and the little old ladies were still creaking—with all of their rubbery, dry tendons, and all of their dry, unlubricated bones; assuaged by the society of scorned harlots; moth-eaten, but still coinciding with the voices, as well as the harmonicas of unobstructed liberties.

Tragically, that's where I observed more human atrocity. That day, I watched a little girl drown in The Twin River of Echoes. At fault, the same little boy that loved her, except he was too drunk to save her life. I called him Flibbertigibbet; akin to anything, or anyone that has ever been useless, drunk, or irresponsible. Others called him expletives, with a great deal of slurs, disgraceful, but still a declaimer that was always shameful, with or without contrition.

From that day forward, he re-transformed the meaning of the word eloquence *into his own century of delusion; privatized, by, through, and with a sad and heavy-heart, as well as an imaginary piano that consoled the vast guilt of his personal disconsolation.*

So I refocused on my own circumstance: of life, as well as death. Self-explanatory, but that was his life, and this was my life. For me, it was the corn fields, as well as the hope of a better solution, every year thereafter. Those were my dreams; by, through, and with the neediest children of God, including myself.

Parlous, prohibitively: I needed sovereignty; for myself, as well as the uniqueness of my own personal lineage, just as much as I needed it for acceptance into heaven, and the little boy needed eloquence, just as much as he needed self-assessment, for forgiveness. As will I, someday, that we shared in common.

Making me the beneficiary, providing me with a much better outlook in life, as well as a better idea on how to intermix myself with the earth's subsoil, creating a better topsoil for the flowery friends of the earth, with a brand new layer of compost. I called it—my sovereign dreams, *interlaced with heartfelt condolences, as well as my deepest apologies; when reasoning died and the world became a much more barren place because of my intrinsic morbidity. Others called it The Aboriginal Platform of Delirium.*

Far-reaching, far-stretched; I couldn't stop babbling, from the extrinsic rooftops of the world, to the wine cellars of hell. That was my worldview, in observance of the mere formalities, adapted in my new realm of solidity, shutting the doors, and closing my view of an old solidity, for now, but reopening my view of human atrocity, with shock waves, as well as an abounding reality.

Articulating a monologue that would help redefine who and what he really was; riveting, but self-indulgent, and always perilous; by, through, and with a five hundred mile an hour dust storm; looming in the sand dunes of the world's deadliest deserts; with all of the sidewinders, as well as the tenants, and the mirages, including the camels' backs.

Long lasting, he was the globetrotter; trekking, trudging, traveling his way through thousands and thousands of miles, with the zebras, and with the wildebeests, hoping to find a single body of water, just like he would travel an even greater distance for a single second of sovereignty.

That was my dream, infested with fleas and desiccated worms, depositing their new larvae into the hair follicles of my brand new haven. Sickening, but that was the regermination of the skin tissue (dermatitis), *as well as the skin graphs of my own mortality, detached and contradicted, but always complementary of the word* metamorphosis, *as well as the most distinct possibility of my own immortality.*

Nullifying, abnegated by the credentials of the brainstorms. Bursting through the extraneous lairs; apposite, those were the irate clouds, with emphatic descriptions of my own sensationalism.

Convulsed and careened, that was the shock of the greatest shockwaves, disbelief, electrified by the unsteady hands of nitroglycerin; shaky, jumpy, antsy, about to blast the earth's atmospheric sciences.

Those were the clouds, ultimately my final resting place. Oft or less traveled by the most persistent pioneers, as well as the most affronted frontiersmen of the devalued West, from the valleys and dales of introspective lore, to the mountainous peaks of the Cascade Mountain Range.

Colliding, those were the subliminal messages, as well as the outright components of my own restlessness and liveliness. Flashes of courage, conceived with flashes of knowledge; all of which were combined by the same expedient levels of bravery, expertise, and becomingness. Synonymous with my namesake, Brazen Maven, clashing with the first five years of my life, quite simply. Those were the personal episodes of aforementioned men.

Futuristically, looking back on the events that hadn't transpired: who, what, when, how, or why. Nobody really knew, and nobody really cared. He was just lucky to be alive and have the opportunity to self-reflect; many years from now, as he often prognosticated; speaking of the present, not necessarily the future, assuming that he will even be alive, more than one year from now, let alone ten.

Impregnation: The Art of Engenderment

Vividly, I can remember thinking back, from the night owls of dusk, until the reflections of the unassuming silhouettes that disappeared. Those were the configurations of the graceful fawns that were drinking water, distinguished and highlighted by the sunrise in the dawn of my fetal voyage.

More pointedly, that's when I was just a flowery, meticulous resemblance of the earth's truths. Wilting, sleeping, peacefully in the nightfall of its universal tells.

Chronicled, on a larger scale, with an even larger version, elaborating the chronological timetables of the selective process, as well as the same rivers of examples, and the same mud houses that were also built on the sinking feelings, with refined walls and self-examination, not to mention my own personal perception of the dubious aggrandizement.

Grandstanding, on the premise of the invented panache. Defensive, but that was the thesis of my own sovereign expedition. Referring to who, what, when, if, it, or why? Self-acknowledging; that was the fate that belonged to someone else, or something much more deserving than I ever was. Exhibiting, that's when I knew that I was always wishful, and I was always optimistic, just not willing to die in vain.

Selflessly, seedless, and selfishly: I don't know the answers to my inborn riddles, but I always knew that I would find the answers to all of my questions. One day, when I finally realize the earth's subsidiaries are just an integral part of the comet's, finite interface; destined to kill us all.

For me, the day was coming. That's because I believe the sky is blue, and I believe the sun is made of fire (gases in particular). *I also believe the earth is not alone, and that there is life on other planets, just like there is sovereignty, waiting for me on the finest side of heaven.*

Much closer to home. I believe the ocean is made of water, and real men are made of hoarse voices, sweat, bad odor; as well as guile, craft, even courage, strength and valor; with pubic hairs that transcend their voices, as well as their reproductive organs. I believe that real men embody a humanistic compassion for the truth, as well as the earth's feminine companions that procreated them, with other men that came before them.

Drivel, drivel—raging, expounding the virtuosity of the world's family trees.

Those were their fathers, and those were their mothers. They were also the sons of their fathers, and the fathers of their own twigs and branches. They were also the daughters of the world's countless flowers. Extending far back into history, and the mothers of all the pine needles, cones, even seeds, but that was the cycle of the world's family trees; when they all finally met their own companions and bore their own seedlings.

Engendering: that was the process of the earth's propagation. That was the subsistence of its own breeding and begetting; with sovereign accents; from the coexistence of the male and female flowers.

Recommending, but reconfirming; that was the nature of euphemisms, when all of my roads intersected and came together, despite the reflections of reality, youth, as well as immaturity. Reclusive; that's when I first learned how to recreate my own fables; legendary, from the fermentation of my own imagination, to the fermentation of a place called The Hypothetical Castle in The Sky. That was the designation of my generation.

In the mist of the world's fogbanks, massaging my floral patterns. That's where I was laved, sousing me, rinsing, bathing, my outlook in life with the depths of the boundless oceans, or a single drop of water. Staring into heaven, that's when I wanted to die because I felt like the world would've been a much better place without me.

Only God knew the reasons why; by, from, and with the cubicles of my own personal morbidity. Withdrawn, so that I could live the rest of my life believing that I was something more bountiful to the earth's arboreal roots; altering and transcending the context, as well as the concept of humankind.

Arguably, mostly against the natural maturation of the physical body. In hindsight, that was the level of his extreme morbidity, and the extent of his deathly thoughts, making him reflect, as well as wish for the smallest denominations of sovereignty, amidst *The Twin River of Echoes*, or the world as a whole, justifying the word.

Metamorphosis

More importantly, that was my morbidity, deterring me from apologizing, for everything that I ever did wrong. Taking me away, from the necessitous road to my own personal salvation; reshaping and redefining my place in history, as the most depressed flower in the history of the world.

Chapter 5

Otherworldly

R *aveled by the perplexity of the squalid chains, for which I could not shed, or ever break apart. I was rewarded with a certificate of meritocracy, as well as a certificate of independence; meritoriously.*

Capricious, my newest and latest prognostication, seeping human sorrow from the corner of my eyes—feeling, foreboding, anticipating the presence of the extraterrestrial beings (who are destined for planet earth).

I can see it in the movement of the sky late at night, stopping for an interim conference at an intergalactic diner on laissez faire, as it pertained to the other planets of the Milky Way.

Giddy: that's where they first started inhaling the interstellar gases of our own galaxy, dispersed throughout the helter-skelter of time and space. Time-traveling from the deepest fear, as well as the deepest anxiety, including the deepest disorders of our own infinity, currently situated on the outermost corners of the diminutive universe, but they were still coming, unmistakably, they were still coming.

Mingy (I was mean and stingy), extracting animalistic data, as well as artificial intelligence from the minds, as well as the brains of the ever-studious bees, through their stingers, and through their educational backgrounds, as well as their life-experiences, making them all reckless but still qualified to give me advice.

Well-informed: many of them died soon after stinging the world's most empty-headed, scatterbrained, attitudinal people. Harebrained, they were also the sacrificial lambs of my own metamorphosis, when they stung me at five thirty in the morning; they woke up the fatherland of such barmy introspection, alerting the motherland of the feather-brained, botanical wells, as well as the seedlings of the rattle-brained, floral swells, applying their own personal venom into the ventricles of my personal foresight.

Declared and personified by the three Is of self-indulgence, dwelling in the extremely wicked subterfuge of—iniquity, illusion, as well as intricacy. Fondly; with a craft of artfulness, bewitched with a special invitation to join the effortless transition of dying breeds. For which I was now a part of.

Chatty, talkative, even more outspoken, in a mental and emotional state; but never pointless; admirably, I was clearly expressive; in my conveyance of the truth, when I didn't know what the truth really was; exclusively through the mental process of otherworldly variables; formulating an immediate need for a motto in life; one that could only be hospitalized by a motto in death, with a grave and debatable argument.

I called it—otherworldly: perturbed, by the gall, as well as the nerve. So I began soul-searching, dignified with a bold and captivating ambiance.

Unearthly, I was plagued by the clear developments of my own profane terminology, swearing with an occult augmentation of the world as it really was, not as I thought it actually was.

Harken, there were a growing number of ambiguous cries from the purity of my own lavish pillows. Flooding my basement; that's where I wept until my lack of diversity overflowed, and I became more diversified; socially, economically, and otherwise, but I was still culturally dwarfed, shorter than most introspective metaphors, but still taller than the elves of the unclear realm, and more sizeable than the miniature misanthropys of the crummiest crag (those were the trolls, as well as the outcasts of society).

Kindly, one of the trolls helped me rediscover the art of portals that had a unique, altitudinous, transitory, disposition about them. His name was Inserted: For My Own Personal Convenience. Contemporarily, that was the self-serving escapade of my own personal relativity, that would help convince me to abhor the adverse effects of such a purposeful divide.

Straightforward, will-o'-the-wisp; revealing more evidence of more substance; bravely: Leaving nothing implied, I looked into the mirror and saw the reflection of a gorging debonair, garbed in plaid suspenders (fictitiously).

Plush: I was dressed to the nines in a silk bowtie (unrealistic); *benumbed by the consternation of the wheedling facade, persuading me to flatter myself* (more believably); *for the enjoyment of the frauds, and the enjoyment of the mounting mountebanks. Gigantic, in their stature, dilatant, elastic, wide-ranging, but always expansible in their girth.*

Cajoled: I was blinkered, narrow-minded; with a tendency to exaggerate the obvious. That's when I made more empty promises to myself that would never come to fruition. Objectified: the land around me was bearing more fruit, as well as nurseries, with or without desirability, or any kind of realization about the daunting peculiarities of my own destination.

Prodded, I was overcome by the articles of pretention. That's when I realized that I was becoming more self-centered. Discomfited; that was the great disability of my own faith. Regrettably, I was tested and retested, reducing my moralistic humility, but improving, broadening, and widening my own personal visions of reality. For what they really were, and what I wish, they could actually be.

Strangely, I saw the reflection of an ever-expounding man that was unbeknownst to me. Yet I accepted him for who he was, morbidly sick, but I always detested him for who and what he would eventually become; an introspective memory with a desired legacy.

Heavenly blessed, heavenly accepted, or so I thought, or perhaps I just assumed—wrongly. That was the man I could never be. Rightly, of or relating to the strongest emotions; that was the only relationship I had with the earth's material animations. For instance, those were the mirrors, as well as the reflections; factually, undistorted, without smoke or smudge; without water vapor, or a doubt of clarity.

More palpable, aside from the species of the bees, and a few of the flies, even smaller amounts of mosquitos, fleas, and insects. I was easily coaxed, manipulated by the political figureheads of the arresting society that always tried to influence other people's way of thinking and living. I called them the human pheromones; some kind of worldly, universal, moral pundits, collectively, or individually.

Plainly, I was castigated, coerced by the vicinity of the interdependent bystanders that were also watching from afar; ever-present, ever-towering.

Lowering my standards, or just my symptoms of paranoia; Lukewarm, that was the aristocratic warmth of my high-mindedness, indicating that I failed unsatisfactorily, with a great deal of remorse, or a great deal of heartache.

Furled, instigating, and inciting, arousing the autochthonous skunks that were also inhabiting the open lands of the bordering forests, spraying me with their own personal itinerary; urinating on the sole species of the monotypic genus Lamprocapnos, valued in the gardens of floristry for their heart-shaped, pink and white flowers. Born in spring; they repelled me, as well as the roses from their habitat altogether. This time I was able to escape; by, through, and with the assistance of the bees.

From this location, there was nothing more deceptive than an indecisive man, that was also consumed by the verbiage of his own bywords, engulfed by the superfluity of his own façade; unable to decipher the intent of his own proverbs.

I stand conflicted, I fall unresolved. Those are the quaffed riddles of my introspective lore, with an un-climactic history of abusive morbidity.

Aver: unfolding, and spread out: he was driven, by a swift and astute conviction; withstanding the test of time: Avowed, Brazen Maven entered the windmills of the contrapuntal melody with an immense endurance, and a worthy agility (a piece of music with two or more independent, melodic lines).

Undefined: that was the counterpoint for which he would be greatly enriched; by the infiltration of his own disparity, as well as a penetration of his own conflictions.

Avouched: in year one of the great escapade, he bent the metaphorical applications of life, adjusting the contemporary beliefs of introspective men (which he was not and might never be).

Changing and rebranding himself as *The Monarch of The Lonely Criterion*, recapturing images of his own resolve with images of his own fortitude; breaking, but still empowering the kettles of his own vulnerability; meekly.

From the start: he was energized by the internal and external dynamics of his own ambitions. Valued or devalued, in just a short span of time, three to four months, all of the acronyms, and all of the bicyclists of the great race were dehydrated from the daily grind of their longing—symptoms of weak-minded auxiliaries.

Then he was sidetracked, readdressed by the old adage of life. That was the scruple that resonated more than all the rest; that was *the will of strong-minded men.*

Undeterred in their quest and in their faith, that was the great pursuit for sovereignty that he could never catch or surpass. Drawing the curtains upon the sunrise, burning down the representational awnings that provided him with more shade in the summer, as well as second thoughts of disquietude that provided him with more burial songs in the winter.

Unearthly, from the time he spent on earth, to the time and place he would leave the planet; graced or disgraced, wishing for a new simile, praying for a new metaphor. That was life as he knew it now; morbidly without sovereignty or respective lore.

En route, he reached for a water bottle as a source of hydration, but that was only the tangible kaleidoscope of his unstructured journey. Vapid, he was drinking sixteen ounces of his own personal despair. Sweating, he was sipping, spitting; dull, insipid saliva through the fermented conduits of life. Inebriating, smashing, slashing, smearing the tokens of his own visual acuity.

Meditating, he used his illusory powers to summon the presence of the infantile ghost. Hurrah, hurrah, that was *Amorphous, The Godchild of The Euphemist.* Figuratively; he was still the trope and the enigmatic figure of an otherworldly phenomenon.

Facetiously, he was indigent but still overqualified. Unkindly, he was the scamp from the medium of roguish rogues. The world traveler of introspective lore, relatively small in size but still large in theorization, about life as well as death, including the architectural vernacular of the world. Including the morbid degrees of right and wrong. Seemingly, he interposed himself with an extraneous, spurious flare.

Thought-provoking: apparently, he was enthralled, subjugated as the greatest rascal of the world's most devious rascals. Trademarked, that was his stigma, related to the gang of doltish simpletons.

Foolishly, those were the scoundrels, imitating, performing indignant rituals, enslaved by the mental images of imbecilic, inexistent life-forms.

That was his imagery, purely but still beautified; antiquated but still pertinent to the underplot of the golden arches, such as the galore of goblins that lived in the gardens of the haunted houses. Obtained; as a gift from the servants of the dormitories in the royal province. Ceasing to exist, imperially, that was the ethereal convention of the loveliest roses the world has ever known.

Informally, in the consequential galleries, as well as the hallowed grounds of the addressed paraphrase, he formed and produced more ideal creations that were inconsistent with reality: imaginative but still delusional.

Substantially, those were Brazen Maven's concepts, distinct from the powers of his own fanciful imagery. Illustrative, but still unnatural, and always unmanageable, making him more unreasonable than a reasonable spectral of the earth, but that was the spatial encounter for the introspective bicyclist, who was riding for more than just the personification of his own personal serendipity.

Ironically, he also had an abnormal element about him; serene, with more details of terrene beliefs and personal experiences that were yet to come in the grand journey of his life.

Unexplainably, he was characterized; by, through, and with the unusual disparities of metamorphosis; attributed to the intervention of supernatural beings; phenomenal, but still eerie, and always superficial.

Categorically, he was sacrificial, yet he was commonsensical, after all was said and done. Despite being painted with shades of gray, as well as shades of disheartenment, that was the great crime, stabbed with shades of wretchedness, and a slow, methodical progression towards death: excursive, with a never-ending morbidity.

Once enlightened: there was an old sullen stream of energy speaking to him, softly by the graded and degraded flowerbeds of The Twin River of Echoes: age-old, age-consumed, with a passel of human body parts that were also spread throughout the main stem.

World renowned: that was the morbid river with an accumulation of dead bodies, dispersed throughout its confluence, as well as the freshwater effluents that were also directly and indirectly connected, with a vibrating phonation; piteously; of the truth, as well as death; of sobriety, as well as insobriety.

Bezonian, Bezonian: The Transparent Ghost of Chanting Legend (that was his phantom title; that was the appellation of the discarnate life); vanished. That was the little ghost that was banished from the titanic wellsprings of the incorporeal world, otherwise known as the foregone, inner light of illustrative creations.

Double Vision, Twins

Implored; he was just a little ghost that begged, and begged, and begged; Brazen Maven, urgently. Unearthed; as The Intermediate Interjection of The Introspective Bicyclist, offering to solve the most complex riddles of his life in exchange for the vibrancy of human emotion.

Irresolute, he was vacillating, but that was merely the formality of the infantile ghost, who was shuddering, diagnosing himself, with a wretched presage, not realizing that he was actually dead until he tried to speak through the diction of such worldly variables, extensive but always entreating immoderate instances of mercy.

Exploring furthermore, he was fractionally illiterate, using the profundity of literacy as a figurative intonation; domineering his ideology. Reconfirmed, those were the assertions, as well as the evanes-

cent forms that were also living; in, and amongst the path of introspective bicyclists.

Festering, oncoming: there was more to the story of his story.
Touted, they were also the espials of the taciturn deplorability.
Fluctuating, fanning the flames of morbidity, with their own personal flowerbeds of woe. Wanting, recoiling in time, without a possibility of writing down their own personal articulations, about life, as
well as vivacity, about introspection, as well as the eternal totalization
of freedom, including the possibility of their own reincarnation.

Liberated, with invisible colors of couth, but still sophisti-
cated with a few good manners, and a few good modifications of
resolution; encrypted, that was Brazen Maven's content; reinstilled,
resoiled with elements of imagery, as well as elements of codification,
tranquilized by the achromatic colors of peace; with or without the
neutral, diatonic colors of fair-minded beseech.

Disguised, he was veiled. Nonpartisan, he was still unbiased,
deciding to unveil his own personal servitude to the chromatic hills
of marvel, raised and appraised with ironic colors of relaxing praise.
Nonaligned; without monomania, or colors of haze, furor, and especially the aberrations of fixed and disengaging raze.

Impersonally; that was the prevailing fad, when he was stripped
and massaged by the colors of comfort, as well as the colors of contro-
versy. Excited or unexcited about the spoiled colors of convenience
and inconvenience.

Obsessively, he was discounted, by the uncourtly, discourteous
colors of partiality with an unsettling discomfort; creating an interior
mess of un-stanched blood, oozing from the internal organs of his
fellow countrymen; when they were all dying around him, and they
were all inhumed below him.

Preoccupied with "idée fixe," said of bleeding to death, he
remained evenhanded by the headstones of the obscure cemetery;
but dangerously detached from the pacifistic mediums of such a
feverish reality.

Delirious: he was walking around in circles, with a fever of a
hundred and one, with bone chills, and a barrel full of aching bones.
Leaving him hospitalized for more than a month of unsterilized

morbidity, where he would be cured or uncured, but not today, nor tomorrow, or many years from now. That's what he had to look forward to. That was the great tractate, shadowed by the great treatise of the great expedition.

Sheeted, with multifarious, polarizing flowers, baptized alongside the children of God, in the enchanted fathom of holy waters: Insurmountable, but still created; by, through, and with the omnifarious creation of tears that once resided with the omnifarious creation of the earth's electric thunderclaps.

Death-defying: by, through, and with the shockwaves of lightning; dead or alive, interred or exhumed, with a sudden attack of elevated horridness. Vanished, he was only able to escape this time by the bewitchment of black magic, or the medium of divine intervention. The next time, he might not be so lucky.

Alchemy, with every legacy, there came an even greater expectation, to surpass the expectations of those that have come before them. Electrified, that was the high voltage, generating automated creations of thunder bolts into the great deluge of the merging thunderstorms. Shockingly, that's when he learned that he could not fulfill the unearthly needs of the slumbering daisies, or the special needs of the ghostly faces from the canopies of the exterior rainforests.

More devilry, lumbering, barging, trundling—down the slopes of inner-directed subjectivity, without being electrocuted. Sadly, he would rather have died that day than live the rest of his life as an introspective castaway—metaphorically, buried by the weight, as well as the weather of the unobscured morbidity.

Dour, a few years later he had a dream that he would be seeing the dissenting provocateur again; imagined, agitating; critically, but safely with an explanatory annotation.

Accelerated, his heart began to beat, faster and faster, quicker and quicker, exscinding the forming drummers of the marching band. They were also nondescript, but still promoting the violinists from the depths of the crackling tombstones anxiously.

Refurbished, he was nourished by the nutriments of his own faith again, as well as the nutriments of his own paranoia. Time and time again, when all other options were exhausted, he referred to the inner-makings of his own personal spirit, portending sketches of positivity.

Enter: The Early Stages of Hallucination

Causing marked changes in the patterns, as well as the marked changes in mood and behavior. Calescent—the equinox was getting hotter and hotter, lit aflame, influenced by the aforementioned seasons with an ever-changing climate. Revolving, routinely, around the universal fireball, as witnessed by the vernal equinox.

Gradually, the summer solstice came and went; blaring, from the viewpoint of the sun. Striking, the solar flares, the size of giants; broiling, sizzling the earth's ozone layer, beating down on his head; depleting him of his strength and energy, leveling his memoirs of such entitlement, searing his scalp and hair follicles; all the way to the doorsteps of the autumnal equinox.

Acute, his physical and mental faculties were also baked. Heretofore, that was the nuisance of the embryonic enterprise, overheated, overbearing at times. Nagging, at the end of year one, he took a nap and rested for a spell before reengaging in the passage of year two. Undiscovered, that was the year of astray and constant dissonance, accompanied by the worldliness of such full-blooded oranges and apples.

Ensepulchered: the end, where could it be? For him it felt like it was on the other side of the world, and he could only wait and see, to be enshrined or to be inurned, even if it meant drowning from the exigency of the world's deadliest, fitful seas.

Ingathering, affluent, those were the hidden treasures of the great pursuit, and then he turned the same hidden treasures into the great imposters with a reconfigured, villainous representation, laced with fruitful illusions of aptly termed propositions.

Naïve but still credulous. Insofar as unaffected, mostly, up until now; then he was corrupted, undermined by the absence of artificiality. Susceptible, as well as unskeptical; that was the audience of gullible fools, as well as the audience that was created by his own credulity, giving him more credibility than he ever asked for.

Heart stopping, graphically, that was the day the farmers in the orchards hung themselves from the tree limbs with a reviled misconception of the truth, as well as their own fate, but especially their own realization.

Wide-eyed, all of this, and all of that was recreated by the archives of indisputability, causing the nucleus of the clouds to begin raining uncut diamonds. Yet it was also dark and cold, inducing more nightmares from the underground world of hell that saw the demon's ancillaries toxify the world's dirt that he couldn't run away from. Yet they were not his greatest demons. They were and always would be his greatest fears.

Chapter 6

Illusions: To Perceive Improperly Is the Perception of One's Own Misperception

*D*isputably, I was eagerly desirous; so I spent the next year living in the clouds; with the salubrious spirits of the birds, and the wholesome, nuclear spirits of the life forces that radiated from the universal trench. I called it—the spatial foss of my introspective spallation (specifically, in regards to physics, as well as the nuclear reactions of the photons, as well as the particles).

Others called it food for the sluggish brain; either way, all of the victuals of the world were widely accepted as the alimentative gift from the universal groundskeepers, to and from the organic fields of the heartfelt macrocosm, blessing the earth with its own celestial donation.

Inborn: those were the provisions, as well as the allegorical groceries, and the people, including the aliens that cultivated them, without bias or color-filled discrimination; so that we could all eat together, splendidly, and cohesively, nullifying the inhumaneness of such an atrocious poverty.

Graphically, the very next day I ate the core of an apple, and the wedge of an orange with a tidbit of my own personal discord; mistaking their contents for the nutritional values of my own foreboding.

Consequently, I blamed it on my own personal euphemisms. The moral of the story: an apple or an orange have never been mistaken for anything else but an apple or an orange; judged by the color of their skin, or the creed of their spirituality, but especially the intellect of their peels or rinds.

I guess that's why I never understood why the human race was any different from the earth's vegetation. My deductive reasoning—the opinions of the fruits and vegetables have never affected the lifestyles of anyone, or anything in the history of the world; as it pertains to the theoretical accounts of the earth's livability.

Even so, I will never mistake an apple or an orange for the wellspring of my foreboding again, as long as any of us shall live or die in the upper regions of the earth's rescission. Puff, puff—those were the clouds; where I have decided to reside, temporarily because the earth can no longer provide me with an unimpeded light, as a direct result of the smog, or a freshwater stream that doesn't have blood in its crippled, long, and pothered ripples.

Smitten, he was afflicted, love-stricken by one of the most interesting, and improbable flowers the world has ever known, with a roseate glitter in her smile.

Prim, I was love-struck, from my humble beginnings, to when I was spiritually grounded.

Unnegotiable, as it pertained to my fear of heights. More spirituous, I overcame my shyness and developed a crush on a flower that I met in the courtyard of a celestial coffee shop. Her name was Ditto, Ditto, Reiterated, with whom I courted and dated from the courteous nature of romance and passion, as well as the curious nature of the world's rose petals that authenticated our own veracity. Including, but not limited to the curious nature of our own legitimacy; questioning my soundness of judgment, as well as my mental health for the very first time.

Sound or unsound: when I was young, I had a deep, meaningful conversation with her about the proponents of self-pollination, a conversation about the multitudinous fruits of life by the balcony of the earth's bluest teardrops, and the balcony of the earth's multitudinous wrought. I called it—the flutter and bustle of my intellectual morbidity, only recip-rocated by the bees, as well as the butterflies, even the populous, but especially the ruby-throated hummingbirds that also attached their nests with strands of spider silk to the smallest twigs and branches, with green-ish-gray lichens.

Airborne, they were all flying freely, theoretically within the earth's habitation. Ecstatic, that was their elation, free-floating, with or without the antiquities of correction and reform, as well as the other species of the celestial body that were making it all more biodiverse.

Maturing, we both exchanged pleasantries. Quixotically, on our very first date I watered down her roots on the dance floor with a recital of our own customized nuptials. Captivating, the other flowers of the world, that's where I wrote her an intimate poem that I only shared with introspective members of the floriculture family.

Fantasizing, we both exchanged our verbal love with a chivalrous décor, cake, as well as sparkling cider, and a Mexican piñata; prototypical of other festivities that were commonly associated with matrimonial vows.

Pictured and depictured, that was our reenactment of marriage. Unrealistic, but those were still the vows that we took with an overpow-ering emotion. Sadly; they were also the vows that we broke, as witnessed by the stereotypical, mischief-makers of God.

Wishful thinking, said of metonyms, that was the great pretense (of or relating to the components of an ulterior sovereignty), *when I first believed in love at first sight from the height of my own ideology, to the fragmentized basement of the earth's morbidity; making me want to become a better man today than I ever was yesterday, or will ever become tomorrow.*

Climactically, preferably, for all of the clinical men and women that have ever lived, but more likely, for all of the granulated sinners that are guaranteed to die.

Grate and triturate—that night, I saw the world through the eyes of the most radiant flower; she was the love of my life after all, pouring all of her love into the metonymical landscape, with a resemblance of my own melancholy, but still atomized by the threat of my own morbidity.

Splintered, we were both micronized, by, through, and with the resemblance of a minced future together.

Summarized, those were just a few of my hopes and dreams, when all of the ebbs and tides of the ocean turned the same color of scheme, with a hot, exploding shade of red, streaming powdery blood, from the empty infinity of her eyes, clouded by the wet and bluest colors of April.

Wieldy, all of this, and all of that was gainful to the long-term prospect of my vibrancy, as well as the indelible interpretation of a brand new sovereignty; redefined by the sunrays of May.

Magnificently, that was our language, when we both reverted back to our roots, with a homogenous style of spells and gels, as well as a medley of more lullaby's and unswatted flies. Heavenly, that's where she first read me a bedtime story, just before going to bed.

Godspeed, in the mornings, when the sunlight pierced through the stiff, pointed needles of the juniper trees. Personified: that's when we were both attracted to pollinator gardens. In short, our colors attracted a colony of insects; insightful to the all-inclusive nature of self-introspection.

Said of the Synecdoche

Encrypted and camouflaged, by my own refusal to accept the very context of her existence. That was the perception of my own misperception. Sinful but still forgivable, when I couldn't tell the difference between the girl of my dreams, and the rose petals of a smoldering, tingling summer together, that beautified her ears, as well as the lobes of her extended family.

Astronomically, she impaled me with her glance, and the most beautiful perspective an utterly astounded creature of the earth could ever imagine, fathom, or ever prefigure.

Batting her eyes, she was more exquisite than the taste of a corpse with a blushing texture of sarcasm; devoured; far and near, deep and wide, high and above the earth's ozone layer, fearfully constant, alongside, within The Twin River of Echoes by the most unmerciful vultures the earth has ever known. More pointedly, and more poignantly; she was also polished and refined, urbanely, with a foreknowledge of my own personal lot; befalling the quests of imperceptible men; presumably, me.

Courtly, she was affable, revived from the ghettos of universal principles. Adulatory, she was also comprised of multicellular organisms that typically produced their own food from the prescience of inorganic matter, but that was the process of photosynthesis; humorous, but still decorative, life-defining, lest I say, life-inspiring.

Ungainly, I believed that I was confused with an aloof disorder; indifferent; as a figure of speech that was meant to be taken literally. Delegated, as prescribed in theology, that was my foresight into the eternal purpose of God; kindled and rekindled, extinguished, but not illimitable or unspiritual.

Unwieldy: in secret, my love for her was heightened with a feverish heat, set afire by the way of a menacing arsonist that was burning up the world. His name was—The Personification of All Inanimate Things That Has Ever Lived on Planet Earth, as well as the theory of gallant, galloping men that were also riding their horses, all the way to the ridges of the great alfresco.

Reignited; my stimulus was set ablaze. Aflame, aflame; fuming with innumerable embers, traveling far and wide, igniting multicomplex fires; to cleanse the sloths of Mother Nature, as well as the egos of kings, queens, and even the demoniacal vultures that were also ruling the dominions of the world with a more sorcerous formation, desensitizing the egos of the planetary system with an original image of themselves that remained unburned.

Reticent: I thought I was unadulterated, so I became more intensified; backpedaling my way into the untraceable graphics of absent-mindedness. Intentionally, all of this was kept concealed, as well as the recent past that could only be remembered; thoughtfully, as well as indefinitely; without clear intention or resolute understanding, of everything, and everyone that has ever continued to elude me, especially the last edition of sovereignty.

Concealed, beyond what I could ever see or avow; activating the hour hands of time, and the same rose petals that would shower the earth with my last words of wisdom, beyond any specified boundary, coming at a subsequent time and stage in my life.

Ergo, while he was racing; spontaneously, his heart and spirit began to relegate themselves, back into the alleyways of the earth's downwardly trends. Sabotaged, allegedly, and incrementally; from which he would never fully recover.

Suggestively, that was decided by the decree, as well as the finalization of the Great Deity. Approved or disapproved, he was foreordained; personifying the nuance of such extravagance; with his statements, and with his declarations; kingly, knightly, but also cowardly.

Strictly, said of stricture, as well as his comments and remarks. Hedged or whiplashed by the sharpest tongues of adverse criticism; in regards to the answerability of his own namesake, knotted yarns, or even the bottommost contents of his transformation.

Bottled with a violent rush of water, written and translated by the fleshless hand of a four hundred year old pirate; narcissistic in their qualities; iced, but still unflattering, and always suppressive, markedly enveloping; not only to himself, but to everyone else as well.

Coagulating, that was the defining moment of the bicycle; in-mixed with the word origins of misunderstood rhetoric.

Characterized by firmness, as well as logical conclusions, I was more pompous, bombastic, even charmed and beguiled by her overall entirety. Sensual, uniquely; I was unrealistic, yet my impression of her was still distended; flattering, swelling, tumid, even inflated with turgid trains of thoughts; of or relating to the philosophy of my own impressionistic views, of her as well as myself, when we were both gibbous (hunchbacked), *bulging my intuitive recognition of the world without either of us. Immediately; unveiling her aesthetic qualities, disclosed for whom and what she really was. More importantly, my aesthetic qualities, for whom and what I really wasn't.*

Cultured or uncultured: *Not as I knew them on the crucial day of our concurrent prognostication; colluding with the same amount of time that accounted for both of our deaths; not now, but someday, vigilant, and hopefully worldly-wise.*

Afterward, I was more demure, reverting back to my unchangeable past, a bad habit that began to itch, haunt, and may never go away. Ultimately, that may be the cause, or in this case, the most probable case for my great demise.

Gloriously, she reopened my eyes to the world as a microcosm of the galaxy; but still substantial to the illustrious deeds of otherworldly beings. Doubtlessly, they were all coming to planet earth. I could feel it in the movement of the earth's designation, anticipation. I could see it in the silhouettes of the incandesce stars, writing their own letters and personal journals with universal explosions, as well as their own exploits, including our own, not to mention our feats; in tandem. We were all going to die, in hindsight or lattermost.

Said of inter, as well as connection; that we were all celestial beings; from another planet, from another time, as well as another thread of life, but we were still connected, somehow, someway, from the beginning of time, to the end of space. If such a thing even exists; maybe even related?

Rotating unsteadily, the earth was strained, undeniably. Fraught, the earth was tilted, scared, gibbering incoherently; just as I was flashing. We were all gleaming. Surely, we were all shimmering. Overloaded, over-awed; quivering from the weight of the earth's gigantic continents.

Expiring: we were all dying; like the condors of the mountainous regions, as well as the seagulls from the oceanic shores in The Middle of Nowhither. Consanguineous, we were all enmeshed; linked to the same marine life that consummated the ecosystem.

Unstable, we were all deeply immersed; those were my convictions, tried and true. Those were my conclusions, painfully obvious. Germane, they were my contents, the abode of the tenants that called it home. Closely related, that was the magnitude of the great embacle; considerably less than enthusiastic.

Waning, darkness ensued, but so did the features, as well as the remnants of torpor. Mired, with episodes of inactivity, causing more intimate remnants of disinterest. Later that day I went to sleep, overpowered by the analogous properties of fatigue and loneliness.

My faith, my faith; my fault, my fault: those were the forces that were halting me. Refrained, but still reproached. Even so I enjoyed the thought of being in love; in my dreams, and in my quest; for now, but not indeterminably.

Drowsy, but not drunk, at least not yet. Tomorrow will be another day, and I will try to be more discreet; for the conceit of the well-born, to the humility of the low-born. Arising, I woke up, reiterating the same sentiments of my foundation; for the upper class, just as much as the lower class.

Regurgitating: I vomited, somewhere in the earth's landfills (with a little female ghost, whose name was Shapeless, Beyond a Shadow of a Doubt), thinking about committing myself into an asylum for the mentally ill. Insane, but that was the process that repeated itself for several more years. Displeased: that was my conduct; fulsomely clear. Shyly or diffident, that was my deportment, unconstituted.

Comprehensibly, collaborated and conveyed with perfectly molded pebbles of rock, as well as perfectly molded pebbles of excellence. More informatively, I signed and lent my name as the Forefather to The Lore of Introspection, as well as the First Son of the World's Unheralded Morbidity. That was me, beyond question. We were one in the same, knowing that prosperity only came in the form of sovereignty.

Encircled: I was reaching, stretching, spanning, but that was the cream of my dream, soaking, that was the bloodstained ink of my closing well; circumferential; touching, encompassing, taking my breath away, one morsel of morale at a time.

Concluding, I was more capable of imploding than ever before. A characteristic of metamorphosis that I shared with the earth's phytology, as well as its hearth; when we were all capable of collapsing back into the same incalculable dimension from which we were once formed.

Reciting, that was the expanse of time and space, inhabited by a population of imperfect people; personified, giving us all life with an artistic style, animated, sparkling. Those were the splendid adjectives of life, as well as the arresting heartbeat of the earth's pomology (the science that deals with fruits and fruit growing); that was the beating of my heart. That was the glitter of the lustrous, fulfilling lifestyle; for some, but not for all, just not me; not now, nor would it ever be; taking it away, just as readily as it did give it away.

Promising or unpromising: that was the structure of my callowness. Untouchable, but always felt; whether I liked it or not; even the most, or the best antirealists could not debate.

Inflective, depicting the colors of omens; providentially.

Clouded or unclouded: all things considered, those were the hosts of betokens; highlighted, cautiously, and fastidiously. Reproducing; they *were all steadily increasing, in sound, as well as numbers, including their strength; making them stronger than ever before, scaring me, halfway to death, or halfway to heaven.*

Frugally; they were also emphasized with relatable colors of prevision, providential, prudent, even familiar, but always regal, and always fantastic; in their nature, as well as their euphemisms.

Déjà vu: I had seen them before, and I would likely see them again; confidently. Painstakingly, they were all veiled. Improvidently, they were inconspicuously missing. Thriftless, they were also wavering in the light. Still motionless, but silent from the fear of darkness; just as much as you and I. Immoderately; somewhere in between, they were imperceptible; to me at least. Instantaneously, I was sullied, re-entangled by the existing soothsayer that came out of the woodworks; whispering in my ear, occurring in the same term of our great disservice.

Chary, he was chivalrous. Connate (allied, agreeable in nature), *yet he was also circumspect; performing, and accomplishing the far-fetched missions of anomaly and anima. Politely, he was surreal, when he left I was bestowed with a brand new light, as well as a brand new grant on my spirituality. So that I could recommence and move forward, not dwelling on the grammatical errors of my past; which had been my history.*

As told, by the modulated voice from within: *More descriptively, I wanted to regain and retain the fruits of my composite. That was the great battle that raged from within; exhibiting, exemplifying; demonstrating a greater, heightened degree of tension, actions, as well as the quality of my life itself.*

Whilst I was excessively particular, but still managed to recompose myself with the same compassion of ancient civilizations. Drawn in, but not fully convinced.

I was headstrong; but still magnetized, lured, reeled in by the fishing lines with a fine, crisp line of understatements, as well as a black, reaping line of overstatements. To her methods, as well as her feministic feelings, to her values, as well as her core emotions; unable to fight off the most native urges of unmentionable men (in this case myself; defamatorily).

Epithetical, she was lustful, that was Ditto, Ditto, Reiterated; with the sultriest eyes, consistent with all of her guiding marks; making me susceptible to the dastardly deeds of changing men. Invaluable to my self-introspection, but those were my alterations, blackened by the littered halls of skirmish and indecisiveness, as well as the littered halls of dishonesty; God forbid; infidelity.

That's what I had to look forward to: as an imperfect man, and those were the sins of unfaithful men. The ones that I chose to walk away from, when the choice was still mine; leaving me beggarly in the alley of dumpsters, like the alterity of categorical vagabonds that didn't know where their next meal was coming from.

Forgiven or unforgiving, memorable or forgettable; preferably the latter, lovingly and foolishly. I was proverbially symptomatic, amorously intrigued by the incense of her rose petals. Aromatic, she was coquettish, much later in our relationship she teased me lightheartedly with the composition of an immemorial love amid the flickering twilight.

Humbly, she was flirtatious; for me that was the truest kind of love, the one that I could never resist, or ever predict, more realistically; duplicate in my dreams, or retract in my nightmares. Whatever the case may have been, it was all translated to the rhymes of poetry, of or relating to the portraits of a distinct reality.

More forthrightly, she conveyed herself with an affectionate circulation of a nonexistent world that helped block out the sun; temporarily, resembling a total eclipse; but that was the unforeseeable obscuration of the earth's heat source, when the world turned black because of my toiled ineptitude.

Tactfully, I was still intact; unsevered, but still immobilized; by, through, and with the quadriplegic limbs of nerveless descent; petrified, but still relieved that I wasn't beheaded in the numinous gallows with all of the earthlings that were soul-searching for their own glory to God, reciprocated by, through, and with the connatural spermatozoon of birth.

This I learned, and I was still learning, that we were all allied, knit together; either by the cotton of concomitance, or by another reproductive cell that was not introduced to me. And we will all die; by, through, and with our very own faith, either by the hand of fate, or through the blighting salvo of spermicide.

For me, it came in the form of peace and tranquility; cordially, with a sovereign stroke, and the painter's shade of vigilance. Those were my perceptions of life and death, and they were my opinions; abjectly, utterly hopeless, but always morbidly inglorious.

Mercifully, I was moiled. Base-spirited, so I reintroduced myself to the whey-faces of reality, which were always fleeting, flying away; professedly, to the end of the world.

Hell-bent: that's where the devil intervened; disguising himself as the definition of REASON *and* MORBID STABILITY, *convincing Ditto, Ditto, Reiterated to turn me away because I was mentally ill, enraptured by the night crawlers of death, morbidly muddled, by, from, and through the people of the earth that still lived in sin.*

Unstable, but we were all thankful, and she spared my feelings, subjectively; explaining furthermore that my eyes were too dark, expansive, secretive for her disagreeable antilogy.

Said of gloom, as well as grim, I was infringing on her flowerbeds that were already untenable, for me at least, full of private matters, as well as personalized trinkets that don't have any kind of room for my morbidity.

Summated: I mortified the earth's plant life, but I understood her point of view and even agreed with her. I just preferred to call them mystic, tranquilizing, if not mesmerizing.

Cheerless: that was my first love, and that was the day I stepped into a new section of my life. With or without her, I knew that it was the best thing for everyone involved; including me, but especially her.

Acutely, that was year two, and that was how much I loved her, with the state and quality of being more ostensible, nominal; even speeding up the hour hand of time; unhesitatingly.

Dilated, my eyes were increasing in size. Divulging; in year three of the frenzied excursion; there was a bundle of more industrious chaos, for which I could not account for.

That's where I sought.

Seeking help from my own mentors, none of which really existed. They were all just phantoms, deceased, and I was still alone; with or without their guidance. Protuberant, on the surface. The air was filled with countless debris of tear-jerking tales, counterfeit goods, bleeding heartstrings. So I ripped them all apart, fast-forwarding to the next chap-

ter of my life, where the real pheromones awaited me, gnawing on the brains, and the cartilage of second-rate thespians; withering away.

If ever, or whenever I finally decide to stop feeling sorry for myself, I may eventually become more dedicated to living a conventional lifestyle. I just don't know if and when that will ever happen.

Slipshod, I was slip-sliding away, as time passed on I buried my memory of Ditto, Ditto, Reiterated. One summer later I fell in love with a female bicycle. Identifying myself with the characteristic traits of masculinity, for which I was now elevated; from the lithosphere of cycling to the stratosphere of the earth's abolition.

Skillfully, I orbited the planet with a gripping tale of insanity that would threaten the viability of my own legacy, as well as the sanity of my own existence; bordering on the edge of the earth's ozone layer.

Released, unbound: I took an exceptional glimpse into the inner makings of heaven. That's where I made a reservation for the remainder of my ineffectual lifespan. Ineluctable, those were the residual effects, when I first started freefalling from the magniloquent bubbles of freedom, to the endless hellholes of my own morbidity.

Caught, by the forgiving hands of a superhero named Irenic Exculpation Man.

That's when I was reenslaved, but not endlessly. Discovering, that's when I also found out there was a way out of hell. I just had to find it. I just didn't know where to begin.

Three hundred and sixty five days later

Inopportunely, that was the year of the firestorm, with a plethora of sentiments, scourged and killed off by a multitude of insecticides; budding, sprouting, clinging on to the peripheral angles, as well as the original neuropathy, surviving the great barrage of heavy artillery, from the cavalry that was armed with poisonous, noxious toxins.

Evilly, that was the manifestation of unbearable, fatal infections; spraying and killing off the most genteel nurseries of the celestial sphere, penetrating the estates of the most profound compounds.

Brusque, brutal; savagely discarded; delineating the sanity of my own insanity. Outlining, reconfiguring the landslides that would help bury the same reclusive hermits, without any kind of human emotion, silencing the prevalence of the firestorms on a cool breezy morning; for now, but they would also return with an even greater fury, and an even greater challenge. That was the depth of my courage and valor.

Subsequently, he was enchained and re-enchained, becoming more infamous throughout the off shooting of his own worldly travels. Labeled, he was slandered as the introspective bicyclist with a questionable deportment. Constricted, he was weighed down by the internal pressures of his personalized expectations.

Anticipation conjured, for the reasons of climbing the most precipitous angles. Those were the hummocks, adding more garbage to the miscellany of the landfills that were already filled with a thousand pounds of personal baggage.

Thinking wildly and irrationally. SNAP. His chain suddenly broke off, creating lunacy; the aftereffect of stupefaction (referring to mania), causing the planarians to go crazy.

Self-professed, he was self-proclaimed; mayhem ensued, followed by alleged vows of madness, but so did his behavior, as well as the general formation of the disorderly mass. Deranged, reoccurring with ascribed paroxysm; spasmodically. Terrifying; he was contracting. Rustling about: With the leaves, and the latest version of his own abominable dissimilarity.

Accursed, everyone scurried about. Panicking, everyone was confused about the bizarre circumstances of formless matter that was supposed to have preceded the existence of the ordered universe; distorted, grievous, sadly misshapen.

From there, he could see the opulence of a much different place, that was the nature of demonology; the lore of the devils, just on the other side of happiness, where he could see the penitentiary, a correctional institution that was more likely to be his home.

Straightforward, will-o'-the-wisp. Endearingly, he was unamused, strengthening his relationship with God, as well as the odiferous velitation that grew on trees; viciously, with or without reliance. He called it—the intelligible certitude of introspective men, coated by the narration of due diligence.

Creaking, he was wilting, thirstily, toppling on the gray areas of shaky ground. Loathsome, in year four of the great escapade he was hypnotized by the pictures of his own infinity, exhuming the dead bodies of the peasants that confided and believed in the power of diversification, as well as the power of trustworthiness.

Blameworthy, he was confined, fizzling out, spellbound by the pictures of his own apocalypse, the same one that was set apart and privatized, especially for him, compounding the fears of his own failures.

Mumbling, he was felonious, at large; wanted for committing crimes against society, as well as his own heritage. Monstrously; he was treading on storm water, with a backlash of demonic dwarves that were chasing him out to sea. Exceptionally; he was ungracious, locked with handcuffs that were made of critique and key repudiation.

Equipped or unequipped: Staunch, he was presupposed, drinking water from the scuttlebutts (open caskets), and then jumping over the lady on the front part of the concocted ship. Seeking salvation, as a recourse; from whom or what he never really knew, as well as sovereignty from the serpentine brooks with an all-powerful sickliness.

Supposedly, he was ailing, almost indisposed of with clumps of rot. Refutative, but still guided by the concentrated beams of majestic lighthouses, emitting two flashes of light every three seconds so that he would not get lost at sea. Until he had to be saved again, rescued from drowning by the superpowers of Irenic Exculpation Man, with a scowl of dismay; released from the proverbial anchors of the ocean, as well as the repetitive, burbling sounds of his own personal exposure to the external influences.

Imagine, said of imagery and pure imagery, experiencing the unfathomable fathom of all fathoms.

That's where the earth paused and stopped rotating around the sun; no longer orbiting, for ten minutes and ten seconds in time. Drawing us all in, closer and closer to the end of the world, making him believe in the transformation of the ever-evolving universe.

Uncommon, but that's where he would ultimately meet his maker, somewhere in the flowerbeds of the celestial gardens. One day, and take a deeper look into heaven; where he will become a permanent tenant in the sonorous equations of a much more likable scenario.

Chapter 7

Puns: A Play on Words

S tochastic (and distinct in kind), involving chance and probability. He was fleeced, pouting, putatively, and presumptively;
without a friend or instructions on how to excavate himself from the
witchcraft of the provisory manors. Alongside; he was accompanied
by his theistic belief, keeping him alive. Dissimilar; when he was
unfriended by the spectacles of humankind. Epigrammatically, that
was the greatest blessing of ingenious sayings.

Transported, he was distracted, postulating with a marathon
runner, and an ignitable scarecrow by the underground landfills of
the horrific underworld (referring to demonology). That was a place
called hell.

Deeper and deeper, that was the infernal machine of the infernal finger; and the overpopulated domain, as well as the right realm
of the wrongful devil; where all of the sins of the Homo sapiens
belonged, as well as the aboriginals of the world that lost their faith
in God. Introspectively, fanning the flames of the most condemned
human beings.

Spitefully, with cantles of pandemonium: that was the incarnate
flesh of the human species. Including his own; for the sins he com-

mitted, and the sins he had yet to commit; where he may ultimately reside if he doesn't change his ways.

Scared and frightfully fearful: on that diabolic night he promised to change his ways. *Buzz, buzz.* Instantaneously, his spirit was reactivated by the succor of the bees (giving him a second chance in life); internally, as well as externally, from the cavities of the earth's most redundant dungeons.

Theoretically, that was the way of his thinking, when he was no longer praying in the company of venomous, academic serpents. Slithering; maneuvering, shedding their skin in the presence of the earth's disbelievers. All of which were commuting, to and from the earth's most dolorous burial grounds.

Witless: those were the agnostics that sold their souls; sufficing the needs of the devilish merchants; contingent on the satanic goods of the devil; who paid for all of his goods with fire and fear, as well as intimidation; just as much as intrigue, with or without a quitclaim message.

Uncompressed: that's when Brazen Maven was dislocated, and then retransitioned in the same lifespan as the annuals, but not dismissed or completely extracted from the boilers of his own hellish surroundings.

Self-cleansing: he washed his spores by the brass tacks of The Twin River of Echoes, with more passages of nitty-gritty, as well as personal poetry, inspired by the flowery banks of dementia.

Enter: The Otherworldly Excerpts of Quintessential Morbidity

Derangement fomented. Isolated: he was singing more children's hymns by The Twin River of Echoes, for the purification of the emasculated soul, and the purification of the rightful equestrians that wangled his trifling deviation. Neigh, those were the severed lifelines of his own in-setting perfunctory.

Lifelong, perfection escaped him, though he never really sought it. From the outset; so did the pedons (three-dimensional samples of soil, large enough to show the characteristics of the horizons; all of them); from the inauguration of rock, to the gravesites of the granular rubble that created the most fallacious craters in the history of the world.

Here and there, everywhere he went. Promenading; they were all about, including the more resolved side of the moon. Far-flung: that was the redoubtable creation of outer space; the redoubtable creation of the universe. Dynamite, but far-removed from the center of the galactic consolation. Yet it was all reinforced; by, through, and with the megalithic stones that honored its adroitness.

Staged, as a prominent point in the solar system to defend the earth from further assault; adept and free from further friction, but not free from further abrasion. That was the landing-place of the dexterous aliens and morbid men, in cohesion with the end of the world. Renounced: with felicitous mention; rejoiced and removed from the microscopic subtleties of the chemical dust; relinquishing himself from the weight of the violent, and the weight of the beatitude that also created the flaming sensations with a mortal existence, as well as the deathly cremations of the earth's botanical heritage with a burning sensation of dwindling flowerbeds; inside of them, all around them. Yet they were all ushered away, with the spigots of the urns, abjured and returned to their ancestry, from the interstellar depths of time and space. That's where they belonged; from here to the liminal line of demarcation.

I foreswear to demit myself and resign. Bang! Three times over, and on three separate occasions he pulled a gun out of his pocket, firing three rounds of hypothesis into the cartilage of his skull, playing Russian roulette underneath a bridge, where he dug his own grave, nearly puncturing the protective shell of his cranium.

Bang—and on three separate occasions he also recused himself from the judgment of life, dropping out of the great race and joining the clan of quitters; that was the way of the impuissance, as well as his suicidal tendencies; showing more weakness, affiliating himself with the regimen of a more shameful introspection. Then; he channeled the embalmed human beings of his own visualized morbidity that were too decayed, and too forgetful to express their own devout sentiments.

Self-appointed, he was the fountainhead of sympathetic intro-spection, half engaged, half-heartedly: In year five of the great esca-pade, he was resuscitated from his disassociation with the hairsplit-ting rive.

Expelled, abridged or unabridged; that was the year he spent exiled in strife; running away from the shadows of his own symme-try; manifested by his own inner-conflictions, as well as the shadows of uncompromised wells. Inexhaustibly deep, they were all strenu-ous, procreating, with antagonistic views; defiled by the implication of his self-indulgence.

Taking heed, he listened to the echoes of the wilderness that were also burgeoning on the outer limits of anything that has ever lived or died; from the signs of the banshees that were wailing away, with all of their feministic qualities, to The Everlasting Ghosts of Yesteryear: in saecula saeculorum.

Uncharacteristically, they were all presented with the same pre-sentiment (bereft: one of their family members was going to die, slowly and painfully, but honorably, with a journal of his or her own reincarnation). Conditionally, as a brief side note in the editorials of time and space: with the grandest rainbows in the history of the world's beatitude.

Trembling at the speed of light, dissipating; literally, from the age of commencement, to the age of reappearance and unde-batable reverberation. Actualized, that was his corporeality. Shaped and reshaped; ponderable, that was his verity, validated by the same deterministic views of the earthlings that believed in the overall cause, or don't believe in any kind of cause; otherwise known as the substantive entities of the world that don't know if they were going to heaven or hell.

Verifying: that was the great retreat for the otherworldly beings that were time traveling from the outermost gutters of the elliptical galaxy, to witness the atomic blast of the great demise. Queasy or un-queasy; he was always uneasy. Feasible, but that's when he saw, met, and was contacted by the brood of chimerical aliens.

Given to using long words that contained an assortment of long, lengthy syllables; they were also known throughout the vastness of time and pace. Classified, and most notably; they were called—The Sesquipedalian Aliens, formed from the island universe in the spiral galaxy; brought forth, from the deepest fathomage of darkness. That was the declination of the un-reckonable star system.

Odorless, they were also fundamentally featureless; wonderfully exhilarating. Well-nigh, they were free from their own perceptibility, as well as the tangibility of their own creation. Initiated, they were all drawn out by a jillion years of insuperable history, but not the flints of outer space; those were the eons that burned away, sucked into the black holes. Swallowed and then consequently obliterated by the otherworldly battles of outer space, for billions and billions of years; never to be to be seen again, never to be heard from again.

Yet those were the aliens, interactive; landing their fleet of spaceships on the front corridors of the monolithic stones, near the lowest register of the bellowing meadows. Adaptive, making themselves feel right at home; feasting on the mangos from the branches of the tropical trees, helping themselves to a cup of introspection, as well as a hearty bowl of metamorphosis; garnished with the same saltine morbidity, as well as a pinch of the earth's pepper, and a taste of Mother Nature's unattainable sovereignty.

Full-heartedly, they sampled "the matured ovaries of the introspective flowers." Those were the avocados; with a green hue and savory taste, as well as the single-seeded berries that also demolished the practicality of the regular universe, with the same statues of memorialized flowers, as well as introspective bicyclists. Those were the reigns of the regnant sovereignty that could never be touched, but only imagined.

For myself, that was the dream; for me, for now, forever, and every day thereafter. Shrinking, that's when I conceded to the clusters of stars that made up the irregular universes. Once allocated, but reconnected by the same agglomeration of time that separated them.

Not limited to, but including; that was my introspective view. By the loamy deposits of The Twin River of Echoes, formed by the same smudge of the sand-filled winds; yellowish and calcareous. Distinctly stated; that was the loess, by the brim of the laterite, as well as the granules of the underlying rock; blackened by the dirty marks of the earth's ferruginous soil; that was the kismet of self-introspection.

Attached, that's when I was interweaved, with the colors of iron rust; curtailed, violated, omitted with lint, as well as the grime from outer space that educated me with a more ineffective perspective. Of life, as well as death; of all things that were possible or impossible.

Yet it was all workable, moldable, somehow, someway, and I was able to clean, sanitize, and mend the smut of my own personal wounds; sewing the articles of my own personal clothing. Efficaciously, seaming my own perceptions, split open by the euphemisms of the world's probability and improbability.

Effectively, the brood of chimerical aliens gave me one of the most inconceivable gifts the world has ever known, that was the gift of knowledge. Presented; by, through, and with a zillion corpuscles that I stored in my memory bank, as a gift from the memory makers of outer space; with a dictionary that defined a zillion words, adding it to my own personal collection of onomastic vocabulary usage, as well as the wordage, and the choice of words that I would idolize, from the origin of time.

Highly recommended, highly appreciated, but always highly heralded. I would treasure that gift from this day forward, in exchange for ninety-nine mangoes, and eighty-eight avocados (one for each of their extraterrestrial children); *allowing me to unleash the strands of grisliness by The Twin River of Echoes.*

Big blue marble; as a turn of phrase; those were the derivatives of the interim visitors; still inoperable to men, but implementable to the women and children of the terrestrial sphere; intersected; by, through, and with the historical examples of the world, as well as the continuance of its very existence, pulverized by the cinders of remembrance.

Partially debilitated, that was the close encounter of the introspective bicyclist. Then he wandered about; mindlessly, somewhere in the clouds, beyond the coastline of the northern continent of the Western Hemisphere, while the rest of his bicycle parts began to malfunction, sliding, pivoting, oscillating.

Damn it. From the slur of slurs, to the inefficacious operation of mankind; surmounting, gradually, over the years. For two consecutive weeks he was also bleached, muted, contaminated with more deposits of depression. Specious, he was nearly censored from writing his own memoirs, by the repressors with an opinion, exscinded without a constitutional right.

Ravished: he was jubilated, pleasing to the eye, but still deceptive to the hosts of philanthropic aliens. Yet he was agreeable to the art, as well as the technique of his own quilted sophism; when he tried to speak to the fallacious pantomimes from the over subtle reasoning of false arguments. Tricky, tricky, but it all made sense.

Somehow, someway; everyone's communication was parleyed without gilded leaves, or an aureate halo from the crowning moments of heaven. Literate or illiterate, delusional or realistic; they still conveyed their own actions, imperfectly, but subjectively. Those were the equivocations, as well as the significant gestures of mortal casuistry.

Superficially plausible, leaving him speechless in the sand dunes of the world's largest desert (that being the Sahara desert, a subtropical desert in northern Africa; covering a surface of 3.5 million square miles), unadorned with a knowledge of his own indecent language. Those were the general principles of his conscience, as well as his own conduct, affecting him powerfully.

Heartbroken, seemingly, he was discouraged; predictively, and to a greater extent. Nonplussed, he was also demoralized. After the aliens left, he was beside himself, flustered, addled. Distrait; he was at the end of the road with nowhere else to go in life, except forwards, breaking through the concrete barriers of abstractionism; or so he thought. Accumulative, his bearings were also defunct. Troublesome, troublesome; but so were his handle bars, steering him in the direction of a more resounding, calamitous debacle.

Reeking, he was commingling, with the biological characteristics of his own desire; solely responsible for everything in the universe that was frivolous. Compliant: he also held himself accountable for everything in the universe that was nonfrivolous; from here to the upper mantle of the earth. Mildly cursing, he became more acquisitive through his utopian moments of maladjusted faculties.

Disproportionate, he was never at a loss for words. Self-imparting; cognitively, he had an utter sense for his own failures.

Essentially, that's when he learned that the most powerful thing in the universe was the intellectualized engine of self-empowerment. Aurified; by, through, and with the stringent wheels that carried him through the most explosive minefields in the history of the word *metamorphosis*.

Poetically Inclined

Scrupulous, I was magnetized, shattered by the punctilious screws that were also derived from the petals of my lovely rose petals, from the grace of my lovely rose petals, to the disgrace of a smirked and oiled rose petal. Selflessly, I grasped for a small medallion that was re-adorned, bedecked by the tropical moisture of such adherence and allegiance. That was the terminal protuberance of my own loyalty; to the world, as well as myself.

Failing—above all, that was my austerity, and those were the cryptic symbols of my repugnant poetry. Inflorescent; for every pheromone that was murdered in the grand domain of my figurative language, there was a transmundane overlay; sealed and varnished, principally from the elements of regicide; as well as the gold tinsels, and the churlish birds that were fumigated by the emerald bullets of homicide. Cut from the courtesy of sapphire crystal.

Bamboozled by the battalion of rooks, serving to exterminate the wildlife from the earth altogether, with all of their reserve, and all of their chemical substances, targeting the animals that were also trying to influence the physiology, as well as the behavior of other members from the same species.

Frantically, they and a small number of euphemisms were also slain by the bureaucratic system of a squelched nation; mummified, publicly shamed under the impressions of the bloody river that had a long history of kelpie sightings, as well as a long history of people drowning and barbaric violence.

Deep blue, as explained. I was dearly and horribly adjusted in the perception of my own misery; distressed from the craft of such a par-

amount, vivid imagination. Ad nauseam, ad infinitum, thy kingdom come, thy will be done. On earth as it is in heaven.

Unprecedented, those were the roses of the uncouth louts that were absent-minded; forcing the descendants of agrostology (the branch of botany dealing with dynamic grasses), to habituate themselves with the more graceless visitors from the outer limits of absurdity, as well as the finer points of foolhardiness.

Brazen, Brazen; rigor, rigor, like the deathlessness of the deification from the great beyond, he stopped intermittingly to lament the asininity, as well as the surliness of the mortal, or the immortal fallacy, with an impertinent discourtesy.

Attentively, he was listening to the misleading, unsound arguments of the ballad mongers. All of which were poorly synchronized. Yet they were all still strumming their wooden guitars with ossified picks that were made of human bone, as well as human stupidity, and human tears, including the documentation of human rights.

Shattering the windows, leaving the wordsmiths speechless, waking up an entire nation; unmannerly, putting to sleep the notion of a more free, liberal, and humanitarian country.

Drinking spirits, with the foam of his sovereign dreams, and the applause of his sovereign speeches; crooning about the iniquitous, boorish barbarians of the imagined land that resembled the degenerate nature of demons (ungodly, irreligious, lacking reverence; of, for, and to God), but that was the encore of comparison and contrast; rattled, endlessly, and always colluding, but still circumstantial.

Bemoaning, he funneled his way through the hellacious streets of short circuiting reinvention; counting, innumerably. Those were the whorls, as well as the swirls; numbered and renumbered, with inexplicable texture of turbulence.

Jostled, that was the sinfulness of the revenants; sending him tumbling, tossing him around, to and from the fatuity of The Twin River of Echoes; mixed and remixed, repelling him with old and new word origins (such as bêtise), defined as a lack of understanding, perception, or the like.

Then he was re-ornamented by the syndicate of rebellious hellions that lived inside of them; otherwise known as the dirt devils, or the concise adaptation of universal exploits.

Provoked or unprovoked, he was salacious, decontaminated, but still, he was stunned by the immaterial pitchforks of the earth's witches that paralyzed him from the wroth of nature itself, as well as the magic spells; sterilizing him from the wroth of the storms that would likely kill him anyways.

Enter: the witches lore, with the capacity to fly and dispense more smoke and fire: swept away by the brooms of the old hags with vile warts on their faces, projected with more vile intentions in their pots of stew that don't have any kind of carrots, broth, beef, celery, or even merit. Brewing more potions of mutilation; outfitted with black dresses, including ancient versions of black magic.

Sinking, further and further into the quicksand pits of his own flagrancy: transgressing, and reducing the pitiable cries of wayward, suppositional introspection, including the pitiable cries of steadfast morbidity, trickling into the age of repressive incumbency.

Remotely, he was imbruted, inhaling false fumes of inconsequential liberties (misleading). And then he exhaled, all the way to the grit of darkness, with the devils offspring, where he continued to reside with the young demons of The Twin River of Echoes, as well as the pillars from the mythological housing of the mischievous imps.

Despicably, he was drought by the albatross; seemingly, that was the inescapable burden of his burden, made of guilt, with or without a scent of responsibility.

My qualm, my qualm; where have the answers to my questions gone? Determined, I leveraged myself out of the soiled belligerence, as well as the muddy waters of the penal indictments. Contextually I was willing to compromise, just not willing to surrender.

Surmised, as a matter of conjecture: *Stern: long before the sun ever thought about eavesdropping on the musical chords of my incongruous melodies, with a bounty of twenty-five thousand arches. Related or unrelated; they were a massive amount of colorful rainbows, rich in minerals, poor in authenticity; bloodstained by the demonstration of the paltry demons that were also vandalizing their spirits, as well as mine.*

Largely considered, they were ill-considered, showing a lack of sense; as well as a lack of insight, including forethought. Nearby, the full flower moon also considered betraying the consonance of my honorable character, of or relating to the spiritual, imaginative world.

Inviting more interpretive context of palaver: *Fearfully, I accidentally mistook a falling star for the end of the world, or at least my own; rethinking the intendment of life itself; touching the things inside of me that I could not possibly touch, or imagine the things outside of me that I could not possibly accept or grasp.*

Nightmares, more nightmares; devitalizing serenity through the process of unimaginable catastrophe.

Frantically, I saw an asteroid explode, and then consumed by the incompatible abdomen of the ocean; sweltering the geology of the belonging seafloor, humbling the experts of the appurtenant ecosystem—with all of their watery eyes; incorporated, by, through, and with one hundred foot waves of grand tsunamis. Annihilation: that was my vista, un-reconciled, slamming me against the proverbial doors of the solar system, with an elevator that would uplift me into the skyscrapers of the farsighted Milky Way; structured with high-flown beams of spire, powered by the energy of ascending morbidity.

Initially that was the gumption, as well as the eleventh hour for the numberless singularities of the cosmos (describing the earth's existence as the Scion of Athanasia); *from the concept of realization, to the lifelines of the oceanographers that studied it; flattening the lifelines, deactivating the endless possibilities of otherworldly possibilities.*

In nautical terms; of or relating to the sailors, as well as the ships, that was their navigational compass.

Commonly, submersing, overturning, and then capsizing the ships of the sailors that were fishing for an immaculate salvation amidst the raging waters of the fitful seas with a cataclysmic, animus event.

Of who, what, when, where, or why. I never really knew the reasons for my knifing morbidity, or the answers to my dispatching introspection, but that was the funeral I attended with a ten-thousand-foot grave. Humbly; that's where all of my goals and objectives were also eradicated from the earth itself.

Temporarily shifting the tectonic plates; resourcefully, shrewdly, but not permanently. Those were the vales of the vales (as it pertained to the world and all of its mortals). *That was the transitional phase of the human race, as well as my own.*

Forthcoming: Insuring more natural disasters, from the valley of purple, redundant tears, to the mountainous confrontations of declamatory oration; and mutating the inner-worldly formations of prehistoric troglodytes, as well as the agencies of modern cave dwellers that were too inattentive, and too uninformed to know the difference between butchery, homicide, and manslaughter.

Haplessly grotesque; murderous, that was the flat out massacre that would never be unveiled; unworldly, dividing man and woman from the beasts of Mother Nature: Comparatively; uniting them with the same religious beliefs that were once related to the certainty of Doomsday.

Irremediable, I was sickly, washing, sanitizing the linen sheets of my own deathbeds. Reclined and reposed, in sync with the abettors of self-analysis. That forenoon, I started thinking, inserting, inferring more solutions to my own self-created quarrels; without restraint and without self-respect, helping bind the story of my surety with a more sturdy, protective layer of prestige, outfitted with the same jewels of completion, dressing me with a tuxedo that refined the image of ineptness.

Extraordinarily: *I began bridging the gap of equality, but that was a costly expenditure of living in the same century as prejudice and inequality; not so extraordinary. Oppressively, I was suffering, differing from the occupants of the insetting malaise, digesting an impressive entrée of undercooked difficulties.*

Raw, I was displeased by the dimples of sour displeasure, with a pound of butter that melted away, with all of my hopes, and all of my dreams, of ever capturing a morsel of sovereignty; retaining it, and keeping it, making it my own; in Perpetua. From a play on words, to a play on impromptu: while he was standing on The Aboriginal Platform of Delirium with an enormity of lassitude: *We were all diagnosed with a terminal light, and an even shorter time to live. Eventuating; I might never get the opportunity to meet the satisfactoriness of life again, but I will always have the opportunity to greet the fulfillment of death; valued or devalued by the vital signs of my maiden voyage; light-heartedly.*

Muttering, I was revitalized, re-soiled, and then re-fertilized; when the interspace of hatred and despicability redirected my directive. Graspable or ungraspable, that was opprobrious; transferred by the streamlets of durable infirmity.

Chapter 8

The Paradigm: An Example, Serving as the Model

S elf-driven, the laborious chase of sovereign dreams reflected upon his own biological characteristics; breathtaking; literally. Inherently; he was also principled, self-motivated. Self-designating, that's when Brazen Maven assigned himself as the soul seeker of the great race.

Now and forever: he was halfway through the understory of his deathlike methodology. Midway, that was the midlife crisis for the introspective bicyclist. Oblivious to reality, just not to life; he just didn't know it yet (a set or system of methods, principles, and rules for regulating a particular discipline, as provided in the arts or sciences).

Disastrously, he incurred a great deal of injuries while bickering with the fleas and ticks, breaking a bunch of light bulbs that turned off his inner-lighting. Combative, he prepared himself for battle with the supporting cast of inner-knights, about to fight the ancient epoch of the earth's demons; ensanguine with the blood of its own morbid history; with or without exception. That was Mother Nature; the land itself, as well as his witness, including the rest of the planetary system that cared or didn't care about the outcome.

Paving the road to recovery, with apologetic retractions, recommended steps, even unrestricted access to the ubiquity of the golden bridges. Built; by, through, and with the prayers, thoughts, and even the love and faith of all things in the world that were ever glorious, as well as the support that could only be used, shared, and found, within the comradery of heaven, with or without taxation; especially, the inglorious, ever-consuming, constriction of blood-filled morbidity.

Obstinately, he defined himself in the arena of reflection and declension. Introspectively; that was the dying authority, his inner-spirit, authoritatively. Still; he was undermined, sloping with a whole new set of inflected forms, and a whole new inflection of nouns, pronouns, and even adjectives, all of which were used to describe the ever-changing definitions of it, he, that, they, and them.

Argle-bargle: that's when his cogitation became more tenuous, restricted with a great deal of modesty, ornamented, but still elaborated with a philosophical inflection of the numerical system (said of grammar, as well as syntactic functions, without changing the form; or in this case the premise, altering the meaning of his life with an array of analytics; for better and for worse).

Numbers (the Double Entendre)

One *was the number of autonomy, the loneliest number since the inception of time, the original sage of diversified mime; from the aboriginal cradle of men, to the impregnation of women's womb.*

Two *was the number of company, as well as the friendliest neighbor of mine; glued with valuable clues, duplicated without a true and abstract mind, as well as the greatest compliment of the number nine.*

Finer than fine, dining with a glass of red stagnant wine, tinctured from the strawberry vineyards with an ample supply of enervated, vintage vines.

Three little, three too many; three big, three too small; three days later, there would be more bee hives; with more keys that unlocked the safe and set us all free.

From the limelight, to the poems that I could not foresee, to the fortnight of the apropos, glee, and wonderful sea; which I could never begin to recite as a historical, stupendous, archeological find.

Typified: those were the storms of the storms, for the grandiose shores of the numbers one, two, and three: For the roses of roses, to the beaches of the world's oceanic shores.

Afoot, afoot—for sure, for sure, those were the colors of the world's solar soars. By default, heaven could wait, and so could the numbers four, five, and even six; as a live and diving rive.

Exhibiting: that was the best part of human nature. Introspectively; that was the best part of me that I could offer the world. My play on words, for some it was enough. For others, it was nothing, if anything at all. Fairly or unfairly, that was my attrition; that was my attribute, my gift, to and from the roots of Mother Nature.

Philosophically, he was offended, by the endless miles of stifling, Godforsaken introspection, as well as the echoes of his own persecution, including the echoes of his own eternal flames. Burning, deeply in the wind, fiercely in the future, quietly in the wet, buried embers of his past.

Slightly impaired: from the kerosene of the midnight oil, where he was crouching in servility, consciously, encountering the lost art of bravery, when the lost art of bravery was with him all the while.

Reinventing: The Innovation of Renovation

Redesigned, he recreated himself through the age of unsolicited aspersion that tried to revoke his glossy, showy colors of valor, as well as a first-rate color of magnificence.

Timorous, he was deterred, briefly, but then he was trivially fearful, coming to the crossroads that were paved and coated with patches of ice; salted and layered with patches of doom, ill-omens, even air pockets of ghastliness.

Cylindrical, the earth was too enlarged for his instinctive relatives, but it was also revolving: For whom the wrath of nature would timely destroy; harboring four natural disasters with an impassibly steep path to righteousness.

Mortified, he was also fortified, but still gaining ground. As a generalization, that was the impractical zenith for the artwork of the introspective catalyst.

Propitiated, that was the metaphorical voyager, orbiting the earth with two wheels and a curvilinear extension on his own roving bicycle, which he affectionately nicknamed *the corsage of piratical buccaneers.*

Inauspiciously, he was tempered by the earthquakes, slammed, jolted, alarmed by the ferocious nature of the world's hurricanes, picking him up, relocating him by the most coercive, emblazoned tornados.

Restarting with a third chance in life to right the wrongs of his antonyms and mortal throngs. Yielding, he was unappeasable; about to be replaced by the pitiless figurines with an irreplaceable point of light. Ruthlessly, he was sprinkled with lighter fluid (flammable), and a dash of salt and pepper by the rodents in the prairies that were going to burn him, and eat his ears, as well as his name. Never again would it be the same, making him lame to the hunters of introspective game.

Those were the pundits of literature, unremorseful; ripping apart his equipoise. Auspiciously; referring to the colossal, most eruptive volcanos the earth has ever known. Relating to their namesake; they were all volatile; in volume, as well as reference.

Imperious, he fell off a book shelf and broke his spine, as well as his cover. Partially exposing him for what he was and what he wasn't; an imposter with a water damaged seal.

For that reason, he was anointed; designating himself the related form of the word—*mythoclast*; reputing himself with the newest edition of estimation. That was the highest form of flattery. Complimenting himself as the destroyer, as well as the debunker of myths.

Putrescent, those were the opposing forces of his eccentricity. Marred, spoiled, and foiled, just one of the many singularities that characterized him with an odd, unusual peculiarity, habits, even flexing mannerisms.

Cringing, he was weak-kneed, flimsy, but still, and always, he will be tenacious. Tirelessly, he was also rebellious. Not initially, but then he became more and more combative through his visions of satanic rainbows. All of which were discolored, demonized by the vindictive, undertones of the world's morbidity.

Trite, hackneyed, successively—he was constantly looking up to the moral compass of life for guidance from the west, rejecting the sensations of the deadliest earthquakes; booming, grumbling, bumbling, with sounds that were caused by the seismic activity from the most treacherous earthquakes.

Smartly, he stayed away from them, re-weighing his options; only to experience the tremors, as well as the aftershocks, bone-crushing, mind-altering. Unevenly tempered, he was effusive, imbalanced, overflowing with unduly demonstration.

Uneasiness made him more prone to repetition, as well as delusion. As a turnabout; he turned to the east, snubbing his nose at the most blasphemous hurricanes of all; possessing the scariest wind velocities that were known to mankind; taking into account the worst possible scenario; that was the aptitude of the mythoclast poseur, with a mirage of unmentionable complicities, as well as a circular impact that was scary, bloodcurdling.

Agape, agape—he lacked reserve. Not surprisingly, there was a reversal of fortune, as well as a duplicitous emendation of the world that had an internal fire burning within it; heating it. Twenty heartbeats later he became more placated. Appeasing himself; emulating the leaves that generated memorable winds of mollification, with greetings from the triangular shapes of the delta, pining away, from the lining, as well as the binding of the lowest morale.

Thinking about death, daily, he invited death to join him for dinner with an open invitation for an exquisite midnight outré, but he was declined, for now. Decidedly, and lackadaisically, he was the pioneer of SELF-INTROSPECTION; assuaging his egomaniacal spectrum. Egotistically, when he turned around, and was struck by the whirlwind of shambles.

Egotism aside; he was unappeased by the single iota of uniformity, separating him from his original civilization. Estranged, he was culpable for his own actions, but not necessarily the actions of others.

Conceding, Brazen Maven changed his mind *amiably*. Yet he was still balancing his footing on the brink of the sacrilegious butte. Unexcitedly; he looked to the south, teeter tottering, but still acknowledging the creases, and the gray hairs of the marauding frontiersmen from the southern hemisphere that had already blazed a trail of commitment in their path, as well as a trail of tatterdemalions in their exclusive catalogues.

Hard-pressed, that was the ejecta and those were the ghosts; these were their stories. Memorialized, they were all trampled, with fiery eruptions, leaving behind a wall of headless bodies that were ejected from the most devastating volcanos; erupting with a burning rage inside of them; harmful and injurious to the introspective soul, as well as the equanimity of his flesh; indefensible to the urgency of his immediate liquefaction.

Unmediated, he also left the imprint of his shoes behind, as a trail of conciliation; only compatible to the foreseeable tragedy of his merciful tears, evaporating quickly on the molten lava rock.

Sensibly, he was well-bred; civilized, by, through, and with the color crayons of eloquence. Courteously, he was agreeable, reconciled, but that was evidence of the great crusade; rarefied, decisively.

Thereof, he listened to advice from the gardeners in the cemeteries that trimmed and pruned his overgrowth, with imagined scissors, ominous smiles, and a gauntlet of more thoughtful consideration, giving special and careful attention to the advice from the haunting nature of ghosts; characterizing him with the larynx of clandestine, unidentified voices.

Anomalous, but still reproductive; multiplying, as a matter of fact, and as a matter of faith, he still distinguished himself from other languages by the unique functions of introspection, as well as the unique connectors of systematic narratives.

Of or relating to the chronological accounts, in conjunction with the language of mucked synchronization.

Manipulated, he associated himself with the infantile ghost, as well as a flower named Ditto, Ditto, Reiterated. Unifying himself with a pirate from the corsair of a lost and forgotten world that only communicated through the mediums of the dead; in-substantiating their existence, until they reached out to the auricles of the living (in this case his own).

Previously unmentioned, that was the hero and the heroin, two euphoric wordsmiths that embodied the spirit of the living; wingless, but still knotted by the ties of memorable happenstance.

Guiltlessly; there was a case of mistaken identity. When the tethered figure of morbidity was referred to—*punctilio: the sumptuous and profound composer of guiding principles.*

Structurally, in life as well as death; Punctilio was not his name, nor was it his motto; in life, or in death, widely recognized for the way he did things and went about his business. That was his modus operandi. That was the way he did things. Inscribed; he was also incised with razor blades, sharpened by the files of extraterrestrial garden tools.

Posturing, he was rebranded with more predictable catchwords, more luxurious prose of literacy, with a cynosure of his own egocentrism. Acclimating himself; he was self-composed with a cleaver and an untethered soul, as well as an unpredictable pattern of inconsistency that was hard to follow.

Purposely, he was roaming, wandering about, aiming for the artisanship of a more purposeful world. Independent of dubiety, he was shielded from the iron fists of inflexible gladiators, mitigated with an enigma of their own ambiguity. Equivocally, that was the hee-haw of the great gewgaw.

Subscribing, describing, and ascribing to the anomaly of the anomaly.

Straightforward, will-o'-the-wisp; this is your direction in life Punctilio, the ceremonial disciplinarian of behavioral patterns and procedure. Embrace it as a new title in life, a personal lesson. Don't shun it. Learn how to vanquish your greatest fears. Learn how to walk through the sludge alone. Only then can you be accepted by the harmonious harps of boldface courage. Run through the fudge alone, demonstratively.

Stop, reflect, and then ponder—only then can you imagine the pain, stress, and realization of unimaginable consequences, and only then can you be denied by the hysterical tittering of the derailing demons with an uncurtailed raillery. Confront your greatest fears in life, intrepidly, as well as your greatest foes and adversaries. Those are the excoriations that are meant to be—pitilessly.

Attempting meagerly, to correct deviation from trial and error; ever conscious of the transfiguring dichotomy.

Wild blue yonder: I am what I am. The universal center of courage and expertise. I am what I am: the heart of the botany. Resistant to attack, verbally, just not practically, or literally.

Subdued, he was conforming to his needs, as a finer point in life. Wriggling, he deviated from his own journey, but that was the pattern that was easy to follow. Inconceivably, but predicatively, for three consecutive months he stopped and wrote a short fictional story called—trauma and triumph (the book of reality as I perceive it, not the book of reality, as I or anyone else really knows it).

Conceivably, for three consecutive months he also followed the guiding principles to his own life as a source of inspiration; renowned with particular detail.

Contorting, he began squirming; flailing, epileptic, in great discomfort; but that was his worldview, in observance of the mere formalities; a common theme in the conquest of his own life, as well as the equal, but separate informalities, as he was perceived by the rest of the world; morbidly forlorn, morbidly unrecoverable.

Signatory: those were the alarms bells that were off-putting, filled with seizures, excessive intemperance; as well as gratification from which he did not derive the greatest pleasure. Analyzable, but still disruptive to the soul; bothersome, without exception, to the rules of widow makers, and to the rules of thumbs. Those were the ingrown toenails of his swollen, inflamed feet.

Chapter 9

Homonyms: Said of *HEADS*, as well as *HEADS*

Mediating, from the lap of heaven, or the seat of hell, with an updated, more pensive, and fidgety rumination. In deep thought. Invariably, he was tediously unvarying, brainstorming throughout the whole process of metamorphosis, emphasized by the shrapnel of morbidity and its antisocial time bombs.

Exceptionally bloodied, scrambling, he opted for the monotony of the north; inexcusably, delving further and further into the wild, rash, and rugged country. Unceasing; he knew the decisions he made today could potentially end in a ruinous, gravitational descent. Clairvoyant, as a remedy, those were the false steps, as well as the falsehood of his own sorting.

Peeking, that was the curious nature of his own solitary confinement, where he was enticed by the elements of Old Man Winter. Frigid, he was by himself, only accompanied by the memory of a four-hundred-year old pirate that was keeping him company; he just don't know it yet.

Hereunto, those were the great mysteries of the great unknown; fearing the hindrance of the great journey that still had to be revealed;

jumping over the skeletal hurdles of his own morbidity, as well as the sporadic impulses of faithless men.

Moreover, those were his only options, as well as the elements of a wintry death sentence that represented the period of his ill-timed decline, decay, even inertia and dreariness. All combined into one new set of rules for finding the greatest common denominator of introspection (that was his subsistence); unable to protect himself from the great wall of abstractionism, or the forecast of browbeating adversity.

Frosted, in the hoarfrost of the blanched winter. The homonym said of FOR and FORE.

Entranced, he was also ensorcelled; for himself, as well as the forefronts of the deadly weather. That's where he was met by a permeated, ludicrous snowman. Heavily built, brutishly loud; put together with three balls of snow, as well as three chuckles of swine, interspersed laughter. Blending in, he was interfused, diversified, but still revolving around the other affixed members of the mutilating snowstorm.

Analytically, that was the repainted portrait of the introspective bicyclist, shoveling snow from the situated summit with a panoramic view of the galvanizing solicitude; aggravating the wintry tornados of the elapsing time clocks. Harshly, with a weeping, heavy-heart. Those were the decisions he made, inverting the cyclones of the external world, continually.

Fathoming in hindsight, those were also the prophecies and the elements of the great unknown, diminishing the elements of his own visibility, blinded by the vagueness of his own necromancy with an official reprimand.

Frazzled, he was domineered by the white out conditions that were too cold and too gelid for the unbecoming protoplasm. Biologically; that was the living matter of organisms, regarded as the physical basis of life, freezing the tissue of his wizardly soul, constructed; by, through, and with the oval spools of his irritability.

Unglued, he detached himself from the mazes of life with the most important provocation. Iced, he was nearly frozen to death by the memories of a much warmer latitude.

Fondly, he began wangling, fighting, sparring and wrestling with the challenges of his own life that were made of fog. In this case, and because of that, he became more impatient; realizing that the struggle of the clime was too intolerant for the introspective stragglers.

The homonym still said of *FOR* and *FORE*.

Long-suffering: for, and out of necessity, he stitched a warm blanket and fell asleep next to the heated coals of a much more peaceful, tranquil dimension; placing himself at the forefront of the resplendent campfire.

Alleviating his captions of morbidity, as well as mortality. Gleaning, he burned away the midnight oil with the brethren of infantile ghosts; slowly, with grapevines of intimacy. Illustriously, that was the beauty of man-made fires.

Sparkling, that was also the beauty of the conflagration. Afore, he began roasting marshmallows, for the clarification of his own believability; satiating his appetite for warmth through moderate degrees of heat, wishes, even prayers; with or without hypothermia, settling in. Unfulfilled, colder and colder; all because of climate change. The earth was returning to the ice age. That was the cycle of its past, repeating itself before his very eyes.

Bleakly but still warmer than lukewarm, hotter than hotter, and still more bitter than bitter; yet it was all sweeter than the taste of truthfulness, brimstone or even fire; comparing the particular times to a two-hundred thousand year old iceberg; shrinking, appallingly, but unforgivably; all the way from the glaciers of Antarctica, to the static state of the Arctic Ocean.

At the highest and most distant point, the introspective bicyclist was sitting on top of the world, juggling three balls of starch, wholeness, as well as time a with a foreseeable end; which was the apogee; putting into motion the scenario that would make the planet unlivable—from here, to the vertex of the amaranthine aeon.

Described as the homonym said of *VERY* and *VARY*.

Heaven can attest those were the sins of mankind, for not responding, and for not acknowledging the end of the world as we may very well know it soon, and may very well never know it again;

manufactured by the way of human beings, destroying its vary surface, as well as the atmosphere of its own livability.

Blubbering, Indispensably, and Incoherently

Expressively, when I woke up my adoration for the mysterious was obvious; endearing. Every day thereafter there was an integration of a new and strange phenomenon added to the ambiance of the earth's epicenter; pressurized, internalized, without a whim or a glamorous sonnet of decompression, or at least varying.

Dateless, I was inhibited by the insects of a different world that now revolved around the harbingers, hindering my craving for such a termless, undying companionship. Snoozing, but I was still advancing in the perdurable stage of my own long-lasting dream.

Pertaining to the homonym said of *LONG* and *LONG*.

I thought big, and dreamed even bigger. Uninterrupted, I was snoring, un-ceased, my persistence remained unbroken. Long-standing, I missed the deadline of recondite poetry. Longing, more than I missed the companionship of a real woman, in life as well as death, which I could envision, somewhere beyond the blissfulness of the fervent fields; from the arcane alleyways of homelessness, to the great abode of my own alliteration; long-lived, long-drawn out, but always cherished, and always deserved.

Referencing the homonym said of *INTERCOURSE* and *INTERCOURSE*.

Alluding, that it was filled and gleaming with esoteric allusions; said of the truth, as well as the intercourse of my life. Wholeheartedly; without intercourse, that was the counterplot for which I was made more conspicuous through multidimensional, comparative forums.

Trending, with a muffled array of aphorisms; misfortunes, as well as the treasure chests of floral beauty that had an alluring fomentation about them.

Down in the dumps, I became more broken hearted than ever before, inwardly, as well as outwardly; unfolding the tale of my own extended yarn; unusually weighty, but momentous. In greater detail, I also became more hardened by the intemperate conditions of the recessive snowstorm; solidifying the significance of my own reluctance to recognize the easily discernible fruits of my life.

Contrarily, at half an hour past midnight, I began sniveling, stargazing over my inner-worldly wishes, bequeathed by the gusts of the swirling winds, as well as the gusts of the swirling ghosts, surging with figments of my own lively imagination.

Afraid for my life: *Banging, slamming, shutting the shutters of my own limpid windows to the world that was colored with an un-blurred translation of the meticulous transposition, as well as a raucous, noisy thunk, reclosing my view of solidity, unpeacefully, as well as my view of palpability; sustaining and maintaining my own quest in life for sovereignty. That was always the goal, the dream that I would never give up on.*

Loudly, deepening the explosions of year six, when I was transparently thin. That's when I became more myopic, already delicately, hazy with a synopsis of my own diaphanous sheers.

Semiopaque, I was over particular, nearsighted, luminous—unbending myself with the poetic verses of contravention, as well as a poetic license of discrepancy. Then I bent over backwards in the age of frustration and dispute without being reputed or despised, negation, as well as confutation.

Undeniably, I was able to see through the things in life that were tucked away by the stone fronts of the reclusive merchants (vocationally, as well as professionally; that was the greatest conflict of interest).

Persnickety, I was fussy, unwilling to act prudently. Defiantly, I was incapable of accepting gratuity from strangers with a farsighted repute. Just or unjust, as told and seen through the interrelationships I had with other essential masterminds of intergalactic space. Meaningful or meaningless, never anything in between, like the same particles of sublunary worlds that were also situated between the earth and the moon.

Undoubtedly, that was my medium. Doubtfully, that was my pleasure, as well as my extremity, but always kind. Unsure; that was the charitable, basic understanding of myself, inferring unorthodox activity from the hollow woodsmen of the forest.

Hexed or un-hexed: they were scorned; transgressing the old growth timber with termites and steel chainsaws, carving a glut of funeral boxes for the fossilized kings and deoxidized queens; with their blades that were sharpened by the annals of intercalated alchemists, producing more knives and weaponry. All of which were forged through the niches, and the columbariums of fire.

Aghast, they were also inciting more ceaseless stares and glares. Sneering, they were simulated by the stilted spontaneity of buying and selling more morbidity than I could ever afford. Reconditioned: that was their obligation to the plant life, as well as the masculine, feministic limbs that were extended from the age of analytical elm trees.

Cynically, far beyond their own history, outliving the same arborists that would also decide and navigate their own fate; correlating themselves with a thousand years of rings that turned into ten million flames of obliteration, as well as ten million hymns of equal but separate extermination.

Burning their bark as well as their primary focus; foregone, as the debris of introspection; that was the century of classified and declassified metamorphosis; the same one that I would probably be remembered by. Derisive, that was the guffaw, as well as the cycle of their own lives; sardonic, hopefully and hopelessly.

Solemnly as a testimonial. Either way, I felt obligated to return their stares; having navigated away from my own productive land without a scintilla of doubt, or a tittle of obstruction; paying homage, as a tribute to the beards of the bees. They were all knowledgeable; far beyond their years, with gray hairs on their legs, and silvery enunciation, spouting from their honey-laden lisps.

Buzz, buzz. Authoritatively, these and those were the terms that I accepted and delivered. Pronouncing, I stated my literary errors. Parenthesized by the bookends of the library, where I met and was introduced to an enormous amount of wisdom, making me a smarter man, with or without intervention from the cosmic fallow that was plowed and left unseeded.

Intimating more homonyms said of MIRTH, and MIRTH alone, just not MIRTHLESS.

Mia culpa, that was my faux paus; with an electrified transcription of sincerity. Said of mirth, and mirth alone, I was distastefully mirthless; that was the cloying of my artificial cultivation.

Ceremoniously, I was partially intoxicated throughout the damnation of my own hysterical shrieking. Now I was the deduction of elusion, attached to the deduction of evasion. Carried away, unhinged by the instruments of flight. Those were the spirits of the eagles, as well as the beauty, and the inner-belief of the pink flamingos.

Unfastening the Voice, as well as the Beauty of My Own Belief

Demanding, I am The Magistrate of Honorific Barrens—seriously, earnestly, but most of all—enduringly, changing, with a soupçon of soup for the inner-spirit of introspective men.

Fiddling, inexplicitly, I was down-at-heel; uncivilized with a boulder of ineloquence. Unkempt, I spent that year drinking excessively with Flibbertigibbet from the glass of tears.

Overqualified, I was dormant, untidy, but even-tempered. Actuated, I spewed more jeers from the replica of my own mirage; sulking in the musty meadows of the wet, boggy grassland; swallowing excess portions of pride.

Ironically, I began to drown in the exigency of my own swimming holes, dunked by the kelpies and the water sprites that conspired against me; intrinsically racking, digging, shabbily with an ungoverned emotion; and an even deeper chasm of my own devastation; locked away, behind the platform of jurisdiction and steel bars. Yet I was still caged and ravaged by the jurisprudence of the fumes from the holistic post-fire with an infernal creation.

Singed—my hair follicles were fried, my eyeballs were bubbling, melting my denotative skin, when there was no shortage of sunshine. Crimping and crisping my demographic with an igneous outrage that paralyzed the epoch of my self-destructiveness; leaving me with a crystallizing effect; tearful, sorrowful, flooding the antechamber of my own self-esteem with a needle nose and a needle point of unsolicited criticism; sharply, as well as my own self-respect, emblematical of the times.

Indiscernible, on the surface, there was a shallow depiction of the farcical coalition. Carelessly, I was inflamed by the infection of the slov-

*enly curriculum. I guess all of this was unusual, but still spreading rap-
idly throughout the fibers of my old-fashioned soul.*

*Sobbing, I began whimpering with the tearful bees that lamented
my recessive sniveling. That's when they initiated me as the honorary bee
of the world's morbidity; extracting the feelings of my own soul, painting
my body black with a flurry of golden-yellow colors, complimented by
the brown bands that varied from dark-to-light striations, as well as a
magic wand for a stinger; fulfilling their avocation, as well as their own
personal divertissement; at the expense of my body.*

*Clarifying: that was the annoyance of the morals; for the monarch
of all morals that analyzed me throughout the engrossment of my own
behemoth journey, daring me to unbutton the internal vengeance that
was raging out of control. In turn, I was spiraling downwards, upside
down, from the funnels of my own execrable vortex; mindboggling.*

Chapter 10

Extending Effrontery

P ro forma, as a cure, from which he spoke, and which he barked, he was carking, uncontrollably.

Disabled, in year seven of the prolonged aversion I was inflated, soaring; high-reaching, high-spirited, with a plethora of zest and enthusiasm; until I began cantering through the spillway of the abundantly littered freeway in the sky; filled with its own elevated landfills of heinous, flagrant, genetic material that clipped my wings and nearly grounded me.

Signified, that's when my brain was expanded (physically as well as mentally), *by the era of miscellany and formal statements; primarily antipathy, prompting the unconventional steeples of the ritualistic clouds with a spotted contrariety.*

Balancing myself, that's when I began walking a tightrope, alongside the seagulls that reinvented me and uplifted my spirit; high above the earth's sea levels, shuffling through the ascetic puffery of the nebulous brumes, with a delayed gait that I could not procure from my own substellar view of the montane world below me.

Repugnant, I was decomposed, incommode, turning to the estates of reality that caused me to fall into a deep, narrow ravine. Superbly or insuperable; that was the gulch of prideful men that were also arrested for stealing the stimulus (thoughts, emotions, and feelings of others), *in the setting of gainsay and boldface thievery.*

Irked and disobliged: that was the year of the burglar; that broke into my memory bank and stole my priceless wealth of childhood dreams, memoirs, as well as diaries. Pilfered, and out of retaliation; that was my history (RETRIBUTION), and those were my memories; taken away from me, miserably with a multitude of divided feelings.

Focusing, I was more discerning. Admittedly, I was even dithered. Forenoon, I plead guilty to the crime as charged; frustrated in the court-room of public opinion. Yet I was diminutive, clamoring, so I spent that year rotting in jail for killing the will of uncompassionate thieves, fighting the swords and voids of my own imbrued conscience.

Glum and hazy, I was in a tizzy, but that's where I lost the battle of inner-wits, hard-fought, but still compromising the battle of inner struggles with an acidic overtone.

Woe is me: that was just one of the many avoidable tragedies in my distinguished life that was coded and secured with visions of wiliness, but loaded and bombarded with more legions of orchards; grown with slews of antagonism, equal but still de-limbed by the same protagonists that once shared an implanted repulsion with me.

Stagnant, he was gaping. That's when he looked into the rear-view mirror, swaying back and forth, inside and outside of the gentle mist. Dumbfounded by the pelicans in the morning. Then he was stupefied by the intelligence of the fogbanks that debeautified his soul, as well as the intelligence of the simplistic symbols of his past, disclosing the image of an aromatic flower that was growing behind him, stalking him, far beyond the corn fields of his own comprehension; freakish in nature with an exotic conformation.

Said of beautification, that was the cinquefoil (any of several plants belonging to the genus *Potentilla*, of the rose family, having yellow, red, and white five-pedal flowers).

Flabbergasted, they were all panellike ornaments that consisted of five lobes, divided by cusps; united by the common denominators of obligation, as well as love and blithe. Yet they were all segregated, sealed off by the swimming holes that sterilized their own water holes of mortification; radiating from the common center of the flume with an atomic, spatial arrangement of blood-soaked morbidity.

Contradictory, opening the sluice gates that would help overwhelm the neighboring glens; sufficed by the artificial channel for conducting water.

Of whom I speak of, by which I speak about, but I do not speak for, nor am I spoken for, as I speak of, only for myself, and of myself.

In reality, all he found was a corporation of sallow, yellowish, brown-colored flowers. Skeleton-like, they were all cadaverous emblems of The Prismatic Glen—gaunt, chalky, exsanguinous. Huffy and puffy, haggardly, replanted and rewatered, raised and loved by the reflection of the craven phantasm from The Blood-spattered Valley of Virulence and Necrosis—unconsummated, with or without their presence.

Vociferate, they were all bawling, routing, shouting; from Brazen Maven's kinship to the dead interhumans of yesteryear, passing away from the dissemination of their own malignity. Disembodied, but still, they were the doppelgangers of the future that would likely suffer the same fate. Forthcoming, that was the elucidation of his own self-preservation.

Doodling, he sketched a new portrait of a lesser man by The Twin River of Echoes. Inconsiderably, he was expurgated, playing an imaginary piano, crying openly by the oceanside of astonishment, where he felt the emotions, as well as the heartlessness, internally shredding his own points of light with abnormal feelings of despondency, as well as recoil.

Intermixing the perfect ingredients for the perfect rainstorm; so that he may be able to one day remember the colors of his spirituality, when the colors of his spirituality were also charred, soot, even tarred, but not fledged or feathered in the spirit of public shame.

The homonym said of GAME and GAME alike. Remnants of the blame game.

Blameworthy, he was self-righteous, becoming more of a liability in the laurels of self-analyzation; but that was the migratory virtue of the great enterprise. Supercilious, that was the game of the greatest game; the one that he could not describe as fair game.

Fleeting and always elusive. Dodging, he was running alongside the contour lines of divine visionaries. Pouring his own bottle of emotions filled with wine and pouting. He began grandstanding with a much more aggressive, hostile attitude on the pedestals of immodesty; but that was the unrestrained saturation of the skull-crushing daggers.

Unrelenting, the rain turned into a symposium of unfledged, promulgating birds, gathering, meeting, and conferring; discussing their own precarious situations; about the souls of the disembodied spirits. Chirping; amongst themselves and amongst their peers. Tweeting; negotiating, amongst the members of the human race and amongst the members of the delusional partisans in the ferly backwoods; proclaiming their own respective ideals.

Cawing, those were the killer birds; suggestively; vaguely, that was the relativity of the world as he knew it then, influenced by the morbidity of the hollow hinterland with a great deal of descry. That was the ferly scenario for the backdrop of the overweening cavalier.

Ho-hum: that's when the surface of the earth and the sky turned black. Egotistically, hinging on the metagalactic darkness of audacity, relying on the kindness of the roses, as well as the spirits of their stems to come together and reestablish the mitigation of peace and tranquility; for the present, as well as the future of humanity; for the earth and for the future of the universe.

Precociously, those were the featherless birds that turned into a flock of skeletons. Deathly ill, they were also eulogized by the preachers of humanitarianism, and the preachers of environmentalism; clear-cutting their own habitat in the old growth forests that were used to carve a glut of funeral boxes for the disembodied spirits of the world.

Plummeting into the fissures of the suspenseful trek, inundated with modicums of leisureliness. Strewing; as the authors of their own deathbeds. Incurious, that's when he submerged himself from the dilemma of the waterlogged subplot; vocalized, that's when he also enabled the erudition of the mote presage.

Narcoleptic, but those were the befitting guests of subjectivity, convoluted by nature, languid, as it pertained to the residents of a place called Prominence.

Chutzpah

Boldly, in year eight of the great exploration, I met a saint in the perpetuity of my own volition; judiciously, anxiously, and innoxiously; while I prayed in the guardianship of the confessionals that were also enclosed and garmented by the house of worship.

That was the rooftop of my own personal faith. Relevant or irrelevant, that year I was distraught, abdicating my own right to live; augmenting my own turmoil in the setting of the indolent, callous millennium, supplicating the Lord with my own right to die.

Supine: those were my suicidal thoughts; again, disregarding the privilege of human life. Conveniently, as it pertained to my own personal interests. Unsmiling, but always stately in the prolusion to the whit of my contrition; caused by the fungi of the genus Fusarium.

Trusting: the saint confided in me and I betrayed the saint's trust with a celestial breach. Insulting, showing arbitrary marks of fusarium wilt; characterized by the damping-off, as well as the wilting of my own spirit with a brown dry rot.

Conscientiously, my name, my resume, as well as my credentials were also withering away. I just didn't tell anyone about it, but that was the earmark of my own erratic behavior, with an excessive transpiration of the truth that would never change the nocuous demons of my own fortunes.

Shamefully, I was insolently rude to one of the most prestigious symbols of deliverance with a heralded divination, as well as an instinctive augury that was conscionable from the assiduous fields of my sacrosanct.

Punctured, I was insidiously cunning, morbidly forlorn; hebetude by oblivion. That's when I met a somnambulant librarian that taught me how to write and articulate my own eulogy; but she was too sleepy and gave me a world almanac, as well as an encyclopedia, since I broke the continuum of time and space for all of the morbid reminiscence I had caused the world in such a short span of time.

Faint-hearted, I was yowling, a sham, but that was my own personal portrayal. Later that day, the yellow and black, felicitous bees showed me how to smile, even after listening to my own transient swoons, all of which were contracted by the subtraction of their own personal wings, as a result of my own personal reductions.

Impersonating the mores of the hoodwinks; shamelessly. Reciprocally, I was reacquainted with the medicinal properties of interchangeable tussie-mussies (a small bunch of flowers and herbs that were not nearly as thought-provoking as I was).

Equivalent or unequivalent: I nearly killed myself for it, and because of it. Hereby, I thought better of it and summoned the Lord for forgiveness. Unwavering, he listened to my extensive supplications, deduced from the fellowship of the enfeebled leaves. That was my own personal thesis. I called it "Cloaking, and camouflaging the fig leafs of my stopgap past"—provisional but still quick and dirty.

Jointly and furthermore—that was the sisterhood, as well as the brotherhood of my favorite compunction. Amnesic, that was my experience with the somnambulant librarian. Her name was Gabfest: the Perfect Tone of Violaceous. The fruit-bearing plum of my own lavender paintings; portrayed as the most deciduous shrub with a pomegranate skin, akin to the women of the world's heliotrope dreams, with a periwinkle smile, and the personality of the magenta, as well as the wry humor of the mulberries.

She was the most orchard, and the most posterity of dialectal. Always exiting the backdoor of reality with a lively imagination. Loquacious, she was also colloquial, demotic, and the most talkative senorita I had ever met, but that's why I liked her because she reminded me of a flower, and always prevented me from fraternizing with the sorority of insomniacs; losing her own memory, shriveling away with all of the other bonsai trees in my museum of dolls and opinions, as well as the paintings in the attics that collected layers of dust particles over the years, cremating what was left of my own memory in exchange for the memories that caused more problems to the palindromes of the earth's forests.

Slapdash, she was institutionalized, hell-bent on restructuring the dictionaries that helped redefine the masquerades of my imaginative sodality.

Psychotically, those were the voodoo dolls that came to life by The Twin River of Echoes, respired by the adjectives that helped describe them. Yawning with a mouthful of insinuation, and a mouthful of more expedient charades, direct accusations that wouldn't go away.

Woefully, they were all exterminated, dissolved into the mud and soil, buried with the company of pseudonyms and other meritorious ethics, as well as the company of over-joyous gaiety.

Relieved: those were the virtues, as well as their ethnicity with a sloppy ploy of foreign translation. Unselfishly; that was the stratagem that gave the rest of the living plants their own water and nutrients, seeds and nuts; making them all hardy again, robust, even jolly with an impression of insomnia; storing their own life's history in the time capsules that were accosted by the rich and full-bodied annuals.

Thereupon and herewith, I was affronted, remitted for my own discretionary ignorance; pardoned and forgiven for my own insensitive, thoughtless thoughts, but those were my actions; and that was my tomfoolery, extending far beyond the range of the perpendicular traverse, cooling down the hearth of the earth that circulated my own anxiety, as well as the angst of the world that circulated my own cognizance. Hereupon, I think that's why I survived the year of boisterous activity, when I failed to realize the error of my own ways until it was almost too late.

Scientifically spinning the compass of life with a dismal, shady forecast.

Follow me, Pococurante (said by a careless, indifferent person, nonchalant), *and I will show you the way to a much more memorable life, not necessarily a better life, just an alternate way of living.*

More inventive, as well as incentive, there he stood on the precipice of his own foretime; enlightening the vagary, as well as the chimera, including the chronological timepieces of his own destination, but that was The Book of Judgment, awaiting him, patiently, by the graveyards of ridicule and indecisiveness.

Graphically, the needle pointed him in the direction of a flock of positivity that turned into a flight of pessimism: Cohesively and contemplatively, they were all shielded, insulated, fostered and safe-guarded by the environmentalists that were extruded from the faction of protrusion and dissension Hereunder: turning the flight of skinless passerines into the cloudburst of oncoming percolation.

Vast and elephantine, huge and immense: Nerve-wracking, pelting the verve. Disturbing, but including the nerves of the most artistic works that had a vivacious incantation about them.

Worrisome, and always unpleasant, causing a great fireside of drastic dread; abrasive, they were all rough and rowdy, but those were the humongous fears of Brazen Maven's vitality. Risqué; they were also the hulking fears of the onlookers in the wishing wells that resembled the ghosts of indelicateness, off-colored death; held hostage by the intimate colors of their own delicacy.

Twisting, winding, turning; indulging their own corroded brains; highly sensitive. He bent the periphery of the warped horizon, molding it into his own personal silhouette, as well as the periphery of a far, far, better place than any man could ever fantasize about.

Forgotten, through a community of feelings; he was deserted, put on display with a texture of his own complexity; confounding the genes, as well as the chromosomes of his inner-makings; but revoking his eligibility to accept the kindness of strangers in year nine of the great ten mile ride, when he became a holy man that was more pious; becoming sacred, even sensational.

Cacophonously, he began rising, out of the day, and into the flowerbeds of fear, where the little demons from The Valley of Everyday Sin did their dirty business; captioned, by the ordinariness of the most beautiful roses the world has ever seen; into the afternoon of a lady named—The Full Strawberry Moon of June. Yet to arrive, yet to be determined, floating in the air; defying the literalness of the earth's gravitational pull, yet no one acknowledged the intellectual divestiture of his proclivity for onomatopoeia.

Objectively, those were the formations of the words that he used to imitate the sounds of the trumpets, as well as the sounds of salvation. That was his gift to the planet; by way of The Sesquipedalian Aliens, as told and lived; by, through, and with their only medium, gratifying him during the musical direction of the most impalpable symphony. In this case he was associated as the referent; except for the children in the crowd that acknowledged he was naturally suggestive, rhetorical, if not reverential.

His idioms: the final stage. When the lights were turned on, the audience began to feel this was the beginning of the end.

Culturally, he was devoured, by the patriarchs with a finite lastingness; amplifying the inevitable declaration of his indoctrination. Rewinding the hour hands of time, arriving on the doorsteps of year ten with a stock of his own pond scum; when he tried to backpedal and rediscover the fountains of his youth under the hot springs of the golden arches.

Drifting, his mind went back into the house of time, but his body stayed in the present, to hold him accountable for the consequences of his aerial flubdub; when he was more pretentious than ever before, with a hash of his own personal nonsense, nearly boiled to death by the queasiness of his own churning; maddening.

Idling, hidden beneath the layers of the earth's crust, there was a parallel image of himself; winded, huffing, and more rigorously puffing. That's where he pronounced himself the archaic scholar of the taxing introspection: For Brazen Maven, that was the tapestry of his own rescission, as well as the indemnification of all morbidity in the advanced stages of life; mastered and re-mastered with a crutch and a wheelchair; symbolizing his ailments.

Agreeably, ten years felt like ten thousand years of strain and restrain. Virtually, he was transcribed, tearing apart the arteries that once conveyed blood from his heart to the conduits of reality; where all of his veins were disconnected from the tissue of his own skin; peeled off with an excruciating degeneration of the Genesis. Extramundane; agonizing, that had to be deteriorative.

Wreaking more havoc: those were the disqualifications of his personal sovereignty.

Outlandish: he was downgraded, by general consent; altered and re-altered. Ostracized by the parasites of society, as well as the parasites of the earth's paradise, chewing on his cheeks, as well as the vocal chords of his larynx.

Displaced: he was bitten, repetitiously by the clouds of aphids (parasitic plant louses). Reforming the pronunciation of his own wording, retarding the fluency of his elocution, having to adapt, whether he liked it or not; one of his greatest fears in life. Yet they were all important pests to the fruit trees, as well as the vegetable crops.

Morose: he was mistaken for the frump of morbid lore; polluting the clarity of The Twin River of Echoes with undelightful arches and dead rainbow trout. Degrading it, as well as himself, with his sinful, suicidal argot, sucking the sap out of his own personal stems and leaves, but he prayed that one day he could reconstruct himself with an even keel temperament. That was his birthright, the one he would like to revisit and never misplace.

Atrabilious: on the next fortnight he was more doleful than the bees that shaved their beards, teeter-tottering on the barbed wire fences of the tolling vexation, indebted by the basements of loneliness and worthlessness that could not be overcome; overloaded; by, through, and with the cargo of poor excuses. Retained, but not committed; upgraded, but not consigned; pestered by the blisters, deconstructed by the same decadence of anguish.

Famished: five days felt like five-thousand years of bloating. Deprived and depraved, five eyesores felt like five lives of incurable depression, as well as an irreclaimable hypothesis. Purportedly; that's when he realized he was no longer the icon of youthful exuberance, without love, and without the ability to be loved; by anything fleshly or unfleshly.

Mournfully, he was frail, due to so many years of senility, aging with an abased sagacity; far beyond his own lifetime. Feeble, he was poor, insofar as impotent, insolvent. Frowzy; he was musty. Illsmelling, he was heavily wearied by the last decade of mind-numbing introspection.

Perfectly flawed, his body was bedraggled, limp, soiled, from the rain, as well as the dirt. Killing his morale, the worst was yet to come; the revelation of his song, that being the revelation of his life. That was the deadpan exegesis of his actual history.

Faithfully, he never lost his faith, despite being antiquated from so many variables of self-examination; unable to recapture the magical foundations of his youth; prideful, but still fading away with great celerity.

Aging, even the term (metamorphosis) was diving, headfirst into the dry lagoons of his own life with wrinkles of fanciful fantasy, recreated by the heralds of hospitality, as well as the heralds of jaded wrinkles that were incised; by, through, and with the gratuitous marks of decrepitude.

Little by little, gracefully or ungracefully, that was the biological time clock of his life, facilitated by the grandfather clocks of time; far beyond his gerontocracy, watered down by the corrosion of his own dilapidation.

Indicative, that was the traumatizing account of the introspective bicyclist; when he was old and began to look for an exit point; from his own body, as well as the earth. Faster and faster than the addendum of the chilling ruse; adjunct to the clauses of his own pontification, exchanged for a cup of coffee and a bowl of intellectualized conversation.

That was the adverbial lifespan of the porcelain vases that provided him with more bygone days of stability. Esurient; he also smelled of roasted beans; redolent, incensed by the smell of fresh baked pastries, and the smell of sovereignty, doting on the dawn of the satiating confabulation.

Overindulgent, he was slender, thin; re-identifying himself as the virtuoso of the ventilating virtuosity; resting on the surface of the glossy countertops, where he was still the subject of pillow talk, yak-yak, and even colloquy, as well as discussion. Flattered; those were the effervescent dialogues that made him feel like life was worth living for.

Zealously, he was fondled. Rapturously, held, petted and caressed by a new generation of little girls that were also accompanied by a new generation of old ladies that once bore their mothers.

Bungled, he was only able to escape this time through the ruse of freedom; predicated by the disclaimer of deliverance; that he doesn't jump over the glassy promontory of the hilltops, expelling his name, but providing him with more recitals of discontent. With one condition, that he be renamed and retitled, happily; there was one little girl in the world that was willing to fulfill his needs, as it pertained to the purpose of his personal journey; her name was—I Love You, with the Fondest Memories; and she renamed him The Sovereign Rose of Morbid Lore.

Out of sight, but not out of mind: Wily, he was only encouraged by the dividends of revisionism. As a form of public acknowledgement; that was the human body, used as a temporary abode for the beleaguered souls of atavism (a reversion to an earlier type); concealing the disparagements of his own life, modestly, but still antisocial.

As a gesture of goodwill, he showed his gratefulness to the murals of the holy establishment. Bowing; for sixty minutes, hoping to receive a special invitation to the peaceful lore of heaven; where he mistook serenity for the end of his life, and listened to the sermon from a talking parrot that was equally baffled by his own episodes of similitude.

Awry, but still dissolution by the subtle dissimilarities; those were the exemplary flowers of metamorphosis; differentiating himself as the head of the homonyms, or the head of metamorphosis; just not the head of sovereignty, or the figurative heads that were lifeless at the bottom of the rock laden cliffs; all of which were decomposing in the trenches of the numinous gallows, prompting more ill-humor than he could ever dream about.

Chapter 11

Adhering to the Word of the Omniscient Lord—Supremely

Huddled and bundled, supremely, with a new pair of bunny ears, next to the rabbit's hole, writing down his own personal excerpts; without a witness or a head of cabbage; without a head of lettuce or an ear of corn. Without an ounce of ink; or a pound of serenity that would help him relax, but he did have more than a handful of tendons at his disposal that he would gladly rip out of his legs, and use to write about the nouns, as well as the stressing vowels; by, from, and about the microorganisms of the world; from the mole hills of the toxigenic landfills, to the end of one day, and the beginning of anew.

Shrunken, he was too small, pint sized, teensy-weensy to be viewed by the unaided eye. Except for, and just beyond the mountain's foot, there was a small congregation of naked mourners that assembled in the bleachers of a small, segregated chapel. Explicitly, they were all in disarray. Unified, they were also the elder statesmen and philosophers of the tightknit community.

Demonstratively, every penultimate man, and every penultimate woman knelt down on their knees. Unpropitious; every stray child (gadded or ungadded), caged or uncaged, every former exemplar also suffered from the same depression as the introspective bicyclist, including their own unremitting bad luck.

In awe, they were the host of God-fearing worshipers that also prayed to their savior; for themselves, as much as they did for anyone else. Oddly, they were the oratory fanfare that began to roar, and roar, and roar, turning the roof of the church into a public gaffe, relentlessly with handclapping empathy, for the subject of the ironical lecture.

Dimmed and sadly darkened, the theatre of luminosity went anemic; until the manes of the lions in the distant pride land turned the color of envy, ghostly gray, with a tonality of their own gothic satire; but that was the source of Brazen Maven's inspiration; when he became a better man today than he ever was yesterday; wisely. He called it "maturity, the missing entre of his life."

Set aside, he had a proclivity for such pristine distinctions, as a chef that fell in love with his own herbs, or as a rose petal that fell in love with his own roots; obligated to confess his sins in the name of the almighty Lord, before he exited the stage of the gospel setting.

Excusing himself, he exited the church, and then made his way through the backdoors of the colorless woods, embalming the bodies of the world that were invigorated by his introspective repartee, as well as the theatrical dramatization of his own life, light, and even love. For him it was called "forgiveness", just as much as expulsion; manufacturing theories of conspiracy, as well as the retaliatory fraudulence of the tiring paraphrase.

Ingrates, More Ingrates

Acclivitous, those were the adult ghosts, blessed or unblessed; accompanied; by, through, and with the infant, younger, smallest ghosts. Even so, that was part of the great hoax; and it was also part of the great imminence of their danger, in cahoots with the likes of the fiendish fiends.

Connecting and then communicating with the casts of universal ghosts; creating more streams of energy, weaving itself upon the ivory keys of the tête-à-tête. Building up to the climax of the piercing return to the grand finale, entailing bigger and bigger expense. Looming in the year of unstructured, public clamoring.

Meteorically, unrestrainedly, he mimicked the hues and cries of the pastor's congregation; alarmed by the aura of the menacing, embroidered horizon. Deafening, even the catastrophic sirens of the bellowing meadows were still lurking in the wind, behind the closets of such gross injustice. Ill-fated, but expectedly, that was ill-timed.

Ill-advised, he was getting closer and closer, to the interval of untold eulogies. Unnerved, he panicked and jumped out of his comfort zone; landing upside down on the front doorsteps of kismet.

Stunned and trivially damaged, he was puny but still standing, highly and mightily; assisted by the invisible ancillaries; deferring to, and accepting the hand of fate; but still rejecting the apocryphal voice from the cryptic symbols of metamorphosis.

Forthrightly, they were all ghostly, embossed, engraved with chisels of dilution, thinning his perspective, about themes, as well as subthemes. Watered down by the itsy-bitsy irony of his own inconvenience, but that was the atrocious prophecy for the foremost authority of his own presentiment.

Aspiring, he was traipsing, walking around in circles, inside of a square box, without the aid of a complementary flower, or the aid of an adjuvant bee to show him the way to a more productive life.

Nearly ten years later, he found his direction in life again; climbing pythonic ladders, all the way to the apex of the prophesized mountaintop; harnessing his own chambers of energy. Culminated; but still terrified by the cantankerous, vulgar sounds of the active mountains, exclusively boorish, with ancient records of their own violent explosions.

Rah, rah, rah, and then the mountains murmured, successfully. Said of lineage, they were all the sisters, and they were all the brothers, they were all the relatives of every mountain on planet earth.

Succeeded by their own records, as well as their own annals of hysteria, including the monographs of residential mutants, some of which were perpetually banging their heads on the granite rocks with a contradiction of their own risible cachinnation.

Nervously; he extended himself upwards and avoided the clefts; head splitting with a tumultuous terrain. Infuriated, he was also bad-tempered, today, but not necessarily tomorrow, he might as well be dead (and he may very well be, were it not for unfinished business).

In search of; that was the never ending story of the great race for sovereignty. By now that was expected, but that was only the bastion of his own conceptualization, trying as hard as an introspective swain could ever dwell on the artifice of his own destiny.

Strikingly similar, that was the purview of his own infamy; where he could see and feel the doorknobs that were made of factory wood from the core of the juniper trees, turning them to the right, welcomed by the lightless mediums of other worlds.

That was the darkness, as well as the link that catapulted him into the wormholes of such a sentimentalized museum, fossilized by the nonphysical world of morbidity, making him the most colorful hyperbole in the universe, for all of time.

Increasingly; he acknowledged the grave markers on the side of the road, inscribed with his name, and his name alone, becoming more discernible as the years went on.

Famously, he waved goodbye to the signs of his own sympathy, paying respect to the spiritual figures that have already expired before him; when he had no proof that any of his enactments actually happened, were real, or ever transpired, but only accepted by the integrity of his own word.

Food for thought: unleashing the ageless crickets, as well as the age old cockroaches of delirium.

Fully depreciated, he was delirious, coming to terms with the words *impugn, impunity*, as well as the *impinging* behavior of the fire-cured, and fire-colored imps. Showcased; that was the full divulgence of the fire wall that was safeguarding him from the spiritual revelation, just on the other side of his hellish quarrels.

Meanwhile, I have to settle for a panel of ladybugs that are arbitrating my future, in regards to the status of my own current residence. Those are my hellish quarters, where I am currently at a standpoint, taking a shower with the devil's shower head, and the devils advocates that are burning my peripheral vision, as well as my temper and dire ire, from the testimonials of pathological liars.

Up above, that's where I belong, that's where I would like to be; that being the more prominent point of heaven; the same point that I would also like to affiliate myself with; the highest sphere of all the spheres with the highest quality of intellectual stimulation: These days, that's what I live for, and that's what I would like to die with; in my coffin, which I value greatly; with images of the utmost appreciation, unlike images of the bottommost likelihood.

Sometimes, I cry late at night because I don't know where my soul will eventually reside, as it pertains to where I would actually like to rest, peacefully; in perpetuity; with the black and yellow stripes of the bees, as well as the prettiest pictures of the butterflies that would gladly grace me with their heavenly, personified eyes.

More food for thought: *With the pollen of the majestic botany, and the companionship of the imperial moths, as well as the rest of their insecticidal camaraderie's. That is the crossroad of my life that has brought me to this point. Where I have chosen the road to liberty, directly connected to the road to suicide, but only I am responsible for delivering myself to the ethereal hands of the deathly wizards.*

Self-deprecating—with sauté pans of buffoonery, as well as a putrid stench of sweet, yellow, red, and white onions that will make me want to cry even more on the same day as my actual revelation.

I have traveled across the country, to and from the terrace of the grave agreement; overlooking the oceans below, from the wispy meanings of the clouds, and the stale calendars of the lingering side effects. Across the great divide, to and from the splinters of the great ocean wide disconnection; equally fractured, but still not permanently separated. That was the grave deterioration of the lizards, as well as my own introspection; equally reclining, but still dormant; with a nom de plume of the slightest reconnection.

I called it—I Have Overstayed My Welcome,
Thanks for the Memories, Good Riddance

To the pseudonym that I could not foresee,
Or ever thought that I would ever misspeak,
And the perished bees that might actually get to
greet me.
One day, with or without the pitch of the world's
tallest trees,
The same ones that were also made of throe, and
fire-resistant bark,
Or ever think that I would ever be, accepted into the
great abode of heaven's lore.
Thanks for the memories; good riddance, and good
grief.

Insistently, that was my poem, to all the men and women in the
world that have ever loved me, and it was also the burial site of my
own reformed imbroglio, commemorated; by, through, and with the
retaliatory grains of the oldest men that have ever lived, or have ever
been entombed; by, through, and with the oldest canes. Of course, that
included the oldest women that were also entombed; by, through, and
with the fondest memories that I have ever had.

Conceding: that was the rebirth of the imperial moths fluttering
about the outer limits of their own liability with the common side effects
of reincarnated affinities; when I was deranged, but not because of their
inner exceptions, or their quality assurance, because I lacerated their
armpits and cut their nostrils in half. Consistently; those were the onions,
not the imperial moths; the same ones that I loved with all of my heart.

Sharply and methodically, I once gutted their stomachs and grilled
their inner-linings, throwing their noses away with the stems, peels, and
even the seeds of the granny apples, as well as the antennas of the bedbugs
and fire ants: Also; my own life-issues that also confirmed their youthful
exuberance (as it pertained to me; unconfirmed, but they were still
the ants).

Damping the spirits, I once hurt their feelings, seeking vindication; but from whom or what I don't really know; at any cost, at any price. So I began ranting, even more; against the rules of culinary schools, and against the rules of conduct in standard kitchens, against my own self will, and against my own imaginary walls that were built with practical tactility.

Perpetrating my right to question the components of ventriloquism; speaking for a wide range of life's metaphors, as well as mummies, dummies and even mannequins that began to speak against me, publicly, as well as my opinions; laced with the same texture as bologna.

Yes, I became so delusional that year that I was outraged by the wild state of my own hysterical laughter; with an endless array of buzzwords, catch lines, even phrases, but not an endless array of brainwaves that would choke the snide remarks out of the most hated hecklers.

Yikes…I was disgruntled, teased by the bitterlings of the pastures that were about to glaze the grains of my own whole wheat leaks with a butter knife and several pounds of bittersweet butter spread.

That's when I yelped—butter-nuttier. Stuttering, that was the curious nature of acceptance, as well as the curious nature of my own lunacy, when I was really trying to say, "Does it really matter? I'm all out of pancake batter." But that was the characterization of my speech impediment, as well as my admission: to God and to the world itself, to every earthling, as well as every alien that has ever believed in these old dying proverbs, leaving me morbidly obese, with calcium in my bones that was also cancerous, perishing from the witty banter of my own morbid illness.

I called it life experience. Others called it.—whatever the reason, or whatever the case may have been, they just didn't accept me for who or what I really was. Sadly confused.

Sincerely, the aspirant of neurotic fantasia

Affecting his status with regard to heaven; on a fair or personal level of equal, but unequal resistance. Hollering; that was the royal command from the vultures that were no longer in denial, but still receptive to the receptacles of ashen-tempered flowers.

Ingested and digested by the wildest scavengers of the world. That was the ever-restless intellect of more, but not less morbidity. Leaving him reduced to rags. Brazen was getting older now, beaten down, clothed with tatterdemalions that were engraved with grunge, as well as a couple more years of tears to go, before the full circle of life will eventually unveil itself.

That was the shredded account of his own remembrance; as it was convenient, to and for the comfort of knowing that he was much better off dead than he was alive.

Toot, toot. That was the freight train, running over his will. Unstoppable, like the runaway caboose from this country's beginnings. Except for, he was powered by the deficient wheels of self-empowerment.

Au revoir; that was the perplexing sign of his own morbidity; running everything over in its path, blowing more hyperbole into the atmosphere from the steam engines of the drastic transformation.

Coughing, that was the diagnosis of his own bloody omens, gravely ill, to and by the month of everything that has ever gone wrong, except for the mint, as well as the sweet, flavored smell of forevermore. Without an extra day, or an extra set of principals; governed by the flowery emotions of the unborn children, unborn flowers, and even the resignation of the emblematical amethyst.

Somewhere else, beyond the funerals of the flowers that began to atone, for themselves, as well as the impressions of the cathedrals that don't have the proper dimensions for a rose-colored funeral box. He was not really a midget after all, but a diminished man, and a figment of his own introspective lore.

Thusly, he was degalvanized, wearing a gunnysack for a vest by the eagles nests of The Twin River of Echoes; pestered by the generic pests of the gospel truth, and the sweat shops of the bee hives that were also working after hours on their new formulas, as well as their new recipes of higher morale, and new batches of honey.

Cresting, they were all knee high in water with a memorandum of their own. Splattered, a few of their own siblings were killed off by the window panes of the earth's roadways; painted, with images of psychosis into the murals of the congregation's imagery.

Swerving, crashing, colliding; they were called—the bee lanes of life: buzzing, buzzing, buzzing, with the beetles and the morbid bodies of knowledge that were also described as the cryptic symbols of their own death.

Limping, Brazen Maven was shoeless, short of bodily fluids, arguing with the dotards and the dodo birds, that were also trying to elicit more philosophical views. For which he, and only he was the truest pundit of all the botanical pundits with a voice, as it pertained to the pictorials of the world with a much better color tone.

Proclaimed, he was plagued by the symptoms of the flu, as well as the symptoms of pneumonia. Those were the respiratory infections of the original sinners, with respiratory problems in the latter days of foreseeable congratulations.

Internally bleeding, he was also blowing on the skeletal horns from which he was born; thanking, it, they, and them, but especially those for absolutely nothing. Otherwise, were it not for them, he would also drown himself in his own self-created pools of blood.

Gurgling at the surface, his lungs were filled with mildew, as well as mild mold, allergies, even a few suggestions from the wasps that would likely scorn the mothers, kings, and queens of baby bees.

Alone at night; waiting to be served at the waiting list of sovereignty. That's when he had the worst nightmares in a long line of impulse, as well as impatience, which was the curious nature of curiosity. Explosive, but still explored, subsequently exploited; explicitly, those were the alliterative sounds of the ticking time bombs.

Dashing, he rushed to the pastures with the cattle, embracing the numerous piles of feces that would also help him grow into a fully developed child of the earth. Distinctly, that aspect of life was partially responsible for who and what he really was; absolutely disgusting.

As he realized, that was the greatest part, and the foremost pleasure of his own reality, but that's what he preferred; the feces, as well as the flies for breakfast, even the urine samples of tomorrow's carnage, as well as the botanical lore of his own introspective finality, satiating his own roots for lunch.

Life as he knew it would never be the same, and no one could ever take it away from him, except for the men of pilfer: Raffish (said of nonconformists); disreputable; said of his own solidity, that was still fogged by the flight of the stimuli; blighted, and clouded by the leopard's sodality, as well as the cheetah's swiftness.

Haggardly, he was consumed, largely by, through, and with the toxic rainwater from the poisonous clouds, making him sicker and sicker from the side-effects of his own terrible illness. Giving him diarrhea, only without the sounds of support, or the sounds of relief; but still received by the same sounds of morbid paraphrase, specifically dictated by the spooks, as well as the witch doctors; mistaking him for a rotten egg, swirling in the toilet bowls of November.

Those were the conduits of his own waste, manually resurrecting his jubilee, as well as his jubilance by the bitterness of December. Coughing, he was shirtless, standing at the forefront of his own communal assembly; inside of the expanding cathedral. With gaudy, showy, cheap and easy to build walls that were also bursting at the seams, but always contrite; with his own convictions; breaking through the walls, even the rafters that began to disappear, from the factors of his own botanical gene pool, interfering with the colorants of perspiration.

Undesirable, he was indescribable; in terms of color, but that was the amalgamation of every morbid man that has ever seen, felt, or heard the ghostly jail cells of under-populated prisons; repopulated by the voices of dead people's resonation, with every ounce of amalgamation. With every ghostly cry that has ever harbored, aided, or abetted the intrinsic fugitive with an informative view of his own morbidity.

Yet he was also green and black, with jaundice yellow; with the same worms, and the same notes, about the possibility of ever escaping the airless realm of his own earthly possibilities. Just like the chemical reactions of outer space, but this was earth, and he was full of mildew; killing his own senses; unshaven, with poor hygiene, as well as multiple tumor growths. All of which were proven over the years; those were the clauses of his rhetoric, underscores, and even the bones and dispirited undertones.

That poor old thing, what did he ever do to deserve such a terrible thing like this?

Out of frustration, he summoned the femme fatale of antiquities, from the rustic outback of the debilitated hinterland. Rumored, she was the femme fatale that would reconfigure his introspectively challenged repartee; by, through, and with the grapevines of a woman's womb; and the womb of his own dignity, but that was The Lady of Prophecy, as well as The Lady of Odyssey. Melted, blended in together, for the depiction of the true definition of amalgamation.

Buzz, buzz. From the factories of the bees, and the factories of the practitioners with more introspective injuries, he was hurt, but still involved with his own metaphorical innuendo.

I was...I was on the verge of sovereign tears. I was...I was on the verge of sovereign lore, forgetting my own metaphors. For this, I have waited a lifetime, and for this; I am still willing to die for.

Dish, dish: those were the rhymes, as well as the wishes. Now and forevermore. I have a new wish in life, that is to meet the femme fatale that will one day help me dig my desired grave, so that I can reveal the revelation, of the real revelation.

Chapter 12

Choices: Revealing the Riddles of the Revelation

S aid of death chairs, lethal injection, as well a public hanging that would satisfy his needs; inhumane, but still appropriate given the options.

Those were my choices, and that was my life; the one that I could not seem to recount; like it was yesterday, but it would still lead me to a better account of everything thereafter.

Bleeding from his feet, more so than his ego; bleeding from his hands, more so than his propensity for healing. Solitarily; he was bleeding from his elbows, neck, ears, even legs; scratching the surface of the South Pole with broken fingernails for an exquisite monologue at the bottom of the world. Experiencing the same elements of sub-zero temperatures as the wildlife with a few plastic barrels of resile; adding more haste and chaste to the earth's misery.

I am not being a good, obeisant, motto, flower, or sacred child of God, fate, date, or even the earth itself. I am being subtracted, divided, even multiplied by the same mathematical equations of life and death. Those are the minimum requirements of the realistic context that I have created for myself; up until now, redirecting my objective.

That's when he came across a morbid prophet that would also help him prophesize his own infamy, as well as the inquisitors of tomorrow. When he would look back and not recognize the importance, or the contour lines of his own shadowy followers.

Freezing, he was disempowered by the temperatures of his own hopelessness; raining cornflakes when he was hungry, raining remnants of flowers from the glamorous veins of heaven. That's when he was more lovable, as well as the remnants of human brain from the tyranny of the world's monsoons, when he was much more deathly than ever before.

Confounded, none of this was binding, and all of its weight was taking its toll on the broadness of his resourcefulness, but that was the gerontology of the glaciers that were also shrinking his shoulders; habituated, by, through, and with the bluish green marbles of time, slow to respond and keep pace with the greatest compliment in the history of introspection.

In regards to race and race alone, he was seedy, untidy, decidedly, the curmudgeon of the earth's crosspatches, or perhaps he was the dudgeon of the earth's botanical umbrage, moaning, griping, sniveling, with the flowerbeds of resentment, with or without salvation. Disorganized and disowned by the same boughs of splendiferous trees that once gave him shade under the flares of the midnight sun.

Drab: there were three residuum little ghosts that came out of the ashes, making their way to the hallowed grounds of the calcified timekeepers, conforming to his needs, as well as his predesigned destiny.

Directionless, he was undeterred. Applauded; the finish line was extended, for him, and for him alone. Rebounding; the race went on, but those were the personalized things in life that could not be prevented, replaced, or ever duplicated.

Bitter, bitter: that was the dungeon of introspective men that could not endure the trials and tribulations of their own everlastingness. Escalating, for ten revolutionary years he hastened, accelerating into the stimulating years of his own introspective account.

Meandering, he used a coarse canvass to paint the unpurified courses of his life with the texture of quivers and mythical lines, even ethical borders that were also transgressed by the same rupture of the pathological divide; one year at a time.

Gripping: that was the tale of unrefined bristles, colorless yarns, depicted by the same unrefined brushes from the haunting nature of inexperienced painters. Theretofore, they were all conceived by the euphemistic nature of concealment.

Horrible, horrible.

Brazen, brazen: *Now that I have exposed myself for what I really am, I must expound upon my own past and tell the story of my untimely departure. Defining, and personifying myself as the inner-conflicted man that was chaffed by the repercussions of his own petulance, destined for the eccentricity of an ominous conclusion.*

Terror-stricken, by a short departure from unity, that was the caveat of the unexpected crash that would likely take him to the first floor of heaven, or the last days of hell, referring to the core of the earth itself as the cardiovascular organ of humanity's wellness.

Those were the repercussions that followed, allowing him to decide for himself, what course he would eventually take in the journey of life. From that moment on he chose the road to recovery, even if it was too late and was inspired by the roads of forgiveness.

My ignis fatuus: will-o'-the-wisp—elliptically. As I look back in a psychological state of retrogression with a fragmented, but higher human conscious level; during the race I devolved and my fruition stalled, infuriating me to the point of no return. Heartfelt: that's when I thought I died spiritually, when I couldn't go back and change the things that I could no longer change. Even so, I was still abashed by the fickleness of my own ineptitude that it made me unabashed.

Superluminal, I was stubborn, delirious, pedaling faster than the speed of light into the ungodliness of my own treasured past. Laughably, I only reappeared in the godliness of my own future with the resemblance of a defunct, morbidly constructed man. Without body and without flesh, inviting myself into the apparent boundary between the earth and the sky. That's where I resided for the longest period of time.

Posthaste, I began spiraling downward. I called it—the disquieting inevitability of my own faith—illuminating the tendrils of the morning glory, as well as the phosphorescent agents of my own incandescent body.

That's when I knew that I was something else, something other than just an introspective man of the world.

Encompassed, I was claustrophobic; enclosed by the framework of the divine lighting, the same one that wouldn't allow me to escape the Lord's name or deny his acceptance. For me, that was the most special kind of divine lighting. That was the hand of Jesus Christ, recoloring the foothills, as well as the footholds of my inner-beliefs, confirming my existence, with warmth and acts of goodwill, as well as love, unmitigated feelings that I could not define.

Entinctured: those were the principles of my own situation, precarious by nature, as well as the principles of my own conscious life that began to glow; picturesque, and richly eventful, intensely colorful; as I look back in retrospect.

Excited about instantiating the farewell to thee; initiating the long journey home, one greeting card at a time, for each of my fellow friends, and each of my fellow countrymen.

Toppled for each of my fellow corpses, and each of my fellow auxiliaries, said of these particular parts, and of these particular accessories, as well as these particular pieces. Those are the keywords, as of then, and as of now... They, we, I, and them, including all of us, and everyone, until everyone else in the world says otherwise.

Fluttering about, I was impinged by the inroads of encroachment. Heart-whole; my heart was throbbing with unusual rapidity; as a result of overexertion. Then it began to pound pervasively, with the imperial moths that died in my own custody. That's when I knew that I was a real sinner of the world; unremitting, down the emission of unbinding continuity, all the way to the hype of the death-defying injunction.

Imminently, that was the impending outcome of my own fruitless life, when I was racing against the most intense shadows of my own history; manifested by my own brain cells with creative ingenuity.

Gorging: I was designed with certain attributes that carried an eloquent charm, as well as a certain tincture of red that embarrassed me. Yet it also beautified me for who and what I really was; indubitable.

Brazen Maven: propelled, uplifted, signed, and notarized. *Intuitively irregular, those were the pros and cons of my own incorporeal flight; when I became more mercurial than ever before, jaunty, sprightly, quick-witted, but always emboldened by the overestimation of my own abilities, as well as the overestimation of my own potential.*

Haughty: my countenance was fairer than fair, but still more beautiful than ugly, spiced with an importunity of salt, pepper, garlic, as well as sarcasm.

Dabbling, I was too pertinacious for my own good; so much that I bolted through the strongest crosswinds, trying to persuade me otherwise to go back to the beginning of time and never return; mind-blowing, discontinuing the lyrical continuity of my own metaphorical usage of words.

Decidedly, I was proactive, operating with an unreserved aggression, maintaining my own course of action. I would never give up on my own dream for sovereignty. Kindheartedly, it stiffened the fibers of my own resolve, questioning myself for the umpteenth time; even after feeling empirical, but still incomplete.

Postponed, those were the latter stages of my life with a smaller amount of improvisation, but a larger amount of nostalgia. Until there was an emergency, and I flinched—tripping, stumbling, upon the most difficult fables of my own life that had yet to be written; horrendously.

Grim, grating, even strident: those were the shrills, as well as the apologues of my remarkable narrative that caused me to lose composure, exceeding the speed limit of rationality, down the retributive roads of compiling, appositional stones.

Rebuke, I was lapsing, feasting on the visage of my own comportment, visibly apprehensive and always disconcerted.

Wincing, precipitated, I gained more momentum, as applied by the laws of motion, as well as the laws of commonsensical theology. Atop the hummocks, that's where I reached unchartered speeds of sixtyfold miles an hour of hellacious temerity; ill-advised, but with the mind-set of ill-willed renegades, as well as the mind-set of unconstrained death wishes. Triggering, interring the ambassadors of my support system: unendingly.

Perilous, I could not withstand the pressure from the parenthesis that was edited by the animosity of the clotting asterisks; hyphenating my own life in review, that was the easiest part of living on the slippery summit, clogging the blood vessels of my own storylines with long, complex, and extravagant words, a life-changing narrative, suffocating the effortlessness of my own perseverance.

Life-altering, Unreformed

Reinventing myself with a shortage of air, life-stopping, as well as insect repellent that nearly choked me to death: Faltering, but not pointlessly. Surcease. I began to yell, or so I thought, and then yell, and yell, and yell, not knowing whether I was actually dead or alive, but taking one step forwards, and ten steps backwards (psychologically, if not physically).

That happened every year for ten consecutive years, until I redirected my approach to the life-size charlatans of the ignominious crowd. Squeamish, they were all still rooting for the deadening spirits of my knavery, killing them off, one by one, effectively.

Cease and desist; then I walked away, with no blood on my hands, and no guilt in my conscience; undeniably resonating. Unclogged, but still endangered; that was the worst possible scenario of the greatest race I ever raced, exploiting the things in life that had been lost forever; like my own memory of love, and being loved in return.

As a footnote: Like the aggregate of past events; outrageously, when no one else could recuperate the grief of the morticians in the crowd that got caught up in the crosshairs of my firestorm. Lethargic, but still watching, taking notes from afar; lest they get burnt; entwining the rest of the spectators that were already holding their breaths, collectively.

Brazen Maven, not so maven; or perhaps, just not so courageous after all—

Imperiled, I was undeviating, gasping for air; the essential commodity of life, as well as a necessity in the fruition of my own aspiration, as distinguished from the physical nature of the earth's animations.

Deprived of color, I was scared, becoming more inanimate than the devilish grins of fire and hell; leaking courage from my own psyche, leaving myself, as well as everyone else destitute, turning our faces the color of lifelessness. Two minutes later, we were all able to breathe again, exhaling, and considerably exasperating.

Afore and before, he was impeded by the variations of idiosyncrasies. Slowed down, he was catalogued by the eminence of the elegant knolls, as well as the inversion of twenty-five thousand foot clouds, bearing down on his own faceless, discarnate soul.

Intensified yet overcome: episodically with a series of goose bumps; more than a million of them, interwoven with the same rose petals, from the same dirt as his flowery origin.

Shrinking, crawling away from his own skin, as well as his own memory bank that once robbed him, and the rest of the weeds; including the rest of the centipedes that regressed back into fragments of nothingness. Inflicted and conflicted by the same twists, as well as the same turns in the road, with the sharpest corners imaginable.

Cutting: they were also cited, relighted with the sharpest edges fathomable. Disjoining, slicing, and then cutting open the thickest biographical accounts of every missing identity. Intrusively but still spurting out pints of blood from the veins of their own dying bloodlines.

Brazen Maven, gravitating towards the lies he told himself, and shying away from the veracious news of the gospel truth (those were the bees, as well as the trespassing fleas). Repelled or unrepelled.

Lawfully or unlawfully, that was my belief when I was still struggling mightily, feeling low, apathetic, deflated. That's when I was uninspired by the context of the derogatory innuendo. Taken aback, unanticipated, with much-needed hope. I veered from the untraveled road, to the same one that I blazed in the dirt roads of my own primordial infrastructure.

Superannuated, I jeered from the natural path of my own uprightness, so much that I imploded, morally with a heart-pounding palpitation. Pulsing, frightfully, and then festering into the cubicles of my own consciousness, replayed in my mind, time and time again.

Excitedly, timidly, that's when I lost control of the bicycle, and the voice of the pirate resonated. In my mind, and in my soul, from as far back as four hundred years ago, long before I was ever born.

Before I was even alive, but that was the concept of my own theorization; that anything was possible, about life as much as death, like I had never known it before.

Exploding, all at once, simultaneously. Perturbed, and slightly impelled, when the transportation vehicles of yesteryear returned.

Expedited; my heart began pounding at more than one-hundred and fifty beats per minute.

Unroused, I was uncomfortable, uncomposed. All of my skin was rubbed away, exposing my organs to the flies, as well as the maggots, representing the buyers, as well as the sellers, and the timeliness of death.

That's when I felt I was dying, and felt reprehensible, and my spirit began to blend in with the rank and file of the living, as well as the rank and file of the dead, more so than ever before.

Desperate, out of necessity; he was greeted by the critical notices with an unresolved matter; burning his spirit with a matchbox of spontaneity. Perked; his ears were also ringing, burning, frilled, ruffled; by the shrills of being killed, and the shrills of being extracted by the predominant colors of metabolism, as well as the erroneous art work that had a schematic preponderance about it.

Inappreciative, he locked his brakes thoroughly with an unfavorable fallout; skidding, scared, rolling for several hundred feet of backbreaking, mind-jarring, declivitous perfidy. Plunging; into the runnels of the abysmal canyon that housed the bloodless skulls and hoary relics of the dead.

As remembered, from the top, to the bottom. That was the anomalous glen, filled with bloodsucking leaches, rattlesnakes, downright, brain sucking sloths; boosting him into the darkest, outermost corners of the widespread macrocosm. Complex, but still interrelated. Painfully; nonetheless, that was the removal of his skin, scraped away, by the texture of his own correction and reform.

Succinctly, he was listless, overpowered by little and no sensibility; subdued by the superior forces of weather-related gales; condemning; denunciating him openly.

Distracted and diverted, he crashed his bicycle into the great wall of abstractionism, with a great terse and verbal brevity, blocked by the road barriers of life; once thought to be impenetrable, by, through, and with the thoughtfulness of such an introspective lore.

Feint: those were the features that were constructed by the obstacles of his own anatomy; spirit-crushing. Beholden; those that observed conferred. Lodged; those that were trapped were also strangled by the hypothetical scenario of such unruliness, reinforced by the typified incarnates, as well as the typified prototypes of his sovereign lore.

Chapter 13

The Revelation: Hallelujah, Hallelujah, Hallelujah

That was the tingling of compunction; when the fore child of Mother Nature was slow dancing with the synchronized goose bumps that once ran away from his own body, and the synchronized water spouts that also provided him with a refreshing ambiance.

For the bluebirds, as well as the feathery friends, and all of their heavenly music, playing in the background of the most placid confessional.

Cleansed and recleansed: that's where the turncoats abandoned him, by the halcyon of the quiescent, tranquil chapel, to face the rest of life's challenges alone; making him an even stronger life force of the earth; revered by the likes of real men that were also climbing their ladders to the apex of the pastoral, amazing serenity.

Unstrapped, unbolted so that he will be able to finish the rest of the great race alone, and celebrate the storm-ravaged victories of life, with all of his reposeful shepherds; the same ones that helped nurture the origin of his metamorphosis. That was the motto; that was the creed of life's most resilient champions.

Smiling with the meekest smile, as taught by the bees, when he don't know how to smile anymore, even after so many years of self-destructive tears. Through the storms, hypothetically, through the crystal balls of presage that could not have predicted the clarions of the most pacific time like this.

On the heels of—he was still chasing the trails of the imperial moths, as well as their own personal destinies. For them that was the virtual conference of heaven, and the virtual colors of life's journals that were also written off by the plumes of royalty, as well as the virtuous tales of his own loyalty, equally baffling.

Buzz, buzz, and the bees came to the rescue. Those were the colors of his saviors, the same ones that would never abandon him in his darkest hours.

Tickling: that was their fancy; surrendering, waving their white flags to the hell bound inferences that did not waver in the windless or furious waves of the ocean. That was the spirit of the bees, that never left him in his darkest hours.

Exposing them for their colors: buzz, buzz. Those were the colors of the hymns, and the truest colors of Mother Nature's choirs. Buzz, buzz: that was their visual, as well as the casual, and the casualties of the Cascade Mountain Range, somewhere in the backwoods of Oregon, where the beavers repositioned themselves, along the rim of the Pacific Northwest, as well as the case of the lowermost rivers.

Trickling with all of their watery eyes and all of their watery landslides, as well as their feelings, from the peaks of the mountains; time restricted; with or without fish. Nearby, the rivers down below were also the tributaries; figuratively, of life's circumstances.

Life-resounding: they were also the arms and legs. They were the aptly named brothers and sisters of The Twin River of Echoes. I called them. The miniature veins of my own waterless soul. That's where I first met the most endearing bee in the history of my life, and I felt the love of her compunction, as well as my own, while we were both becoming more intimate in the grandest rosebushes of life.

Of this I remember, slow dancing with an old wooden spoon in our mouths, and I danced with an old hope that I could not extradite from my own mouth, dipped with honey and cinnamon by the old wooden premise of life and death. In a bar that was filled with gibberish, and buggy-eyed patrons. All of which were speaking with a wide array of inebriated metaphors.

None of which paid for their drinks, but still managed to purge in the sinks of the sunken, wayward ships, boats, even modules, as well as the sons of their dead fathers that were the best brothers of their greatly exaggerated sisters.

Caressed, she held me in her tiny, spiny arms. Sleeveless, but still prickly and dangerous. So I had to be careful that I don't cut myself, while whispering pine needles of sweet nothing's into her finely crafted ears. That's when I danced, and knew that I loved her, we just weren't compatible. For she was a bee and gave me the impression that I was always a rose.

Outside, the dry brush was rolling together; into new tumbleweeds that came to rest by the barns of the cattle feed. That's when I knew that I was going to become the ultimate seed of sovereign beads, once and for all. I am—I am going to achieve my dreams.

Harmless, but still expressing their invaluable sentiments, written and defined by the pithy meanings of such wistfulness. Nightly, his life was derived from the dimension of a more nocuous, conjectural speculation.

Brazen Maven; the deliberation of bestowal, to compare, consult, discuss, and even communicate; imparting his own inner-thoughts, as well as his inner-opinions, beliefs, and even colors of world peace.

Undressed physically but still morbid and dressed for dinner guests. Those were the arms, as well as the fingers; including the legs, feet, toes, and even the fingernails of time. Clipped away by The Everlasting Ghosts of Yesteryear; manicuring, pedicuring his own nails and toenails, as well as the fusty smell of morbidity.

Heightened: those were the colors of his own spirituality, growth, as well as belief. Those were the colors of his own sovereignty, that were also never really his, but only wished for, in the superlative context of something that may or may not ever find its way to the sovereign doorsteps of love and finality.

Upon impact: I was tangled in the bottomless prism of flesh-eating insects, aching with great constraint, enduring more severe punishment as time went on. And as time went on, I was also famished; hungry, or at least I remember stealing a bread crumb from the army of ants. Angered, they all tried to bite me so I ate a few of them instead.

Floating freely, allowing me to drift into the ethos of my own exploration. Innocuous, but still unhinging the buzzards, and the crows that were circling above my head, as well as the pernicious gateways to the flowerbeds with a more favorable, wholehearted piece of my indebtedness.

Unaware, I was still wishing, praying, for the slightest marvel of eternal liberation; losing consciousness, for twenty-four consecutive hours. I was comatose, unresponsive, left for dead, until I was reintroduced to life by the aide of an angelic visualization.

Uplifted, I felt assuaged. For who and what I really was, metamorphosed. Yet the fabric of my own soul was still lonesome, weeping, sobbing, for a flowery garden, as well as a flowery bed, and a plenary of comfort and great distrain.

Thoroughgoing, my immune system was weakened, even cracking my spirit. My veins were dilated from the effects of age, as well as the effects of my own in-setting infirmity, depleting my ability to fight off the world's deadliest diseases.

Thought-provoking: reformed or unreformed, I was still dying; undoubtedly, I was dying and I knew it, but I was okay with it because I didn't want to live anymore under the terms, or the conditions that were provided, to, by, and for me.

Yearning…through the thick foliage of life, with a prelude to the tzimmes (the fuss, an uproar, a hullabaloo).

Extended upward: I wondered about the natural powers that were also ascribed to man as opposed to woman. Curiously; I regained more consciousness from the calamity of the vertical fallout; introspectively at least, but still self-critical of myself, as well as the sovereignty of the world as a whole, but not privately.

Self-attributed: that's when I began to assert more discredit, as well as impute, implementing blame with shreds of chide, enunciating the pellucid, faulty reproach of despicable human beings, as well as the pro-

pensity for inhumaneness; making myself the object of their scorn, as well as my own; contemptuously, if not pitifully.

Un-alert, my eyes were rolling to the back of my head; my brain was concussed, and I was floundering, thoroughly disoriented. Assaulted, I was nauseated by the empty vaults, as well as the empty banks of my own memories. Thickening the plot, that's where I developed a deadly case of gangrene; from the elements of hypothermia, and the elements of time, as well as the elements of my own physiology, inherently.

Finishing and taking care of my own personal affairs, as a personal preference. The solution—permanently disabling my own introspection, from that day forward, until the last day that I will ever live on earth.

Ethereally, that was preferable; when I cross the liminal line of demarcation that has no boundaries. That's where I mourned the loss of my own perspective. Hospitalized, treated by the doctors, and the dictatorial nurses of father time.

Both of my legs were amputated. Heartlessly, I could no longer walk normally, so I belly crawled through fifty kilometers of slough, all the way to the sorcery of the feministic holograms.

Saintly or unsaintly, they were all libidinous, but still lived within my earthly realm, full of lust; irresistibly attractive women; lewd, winking at me with lascivious gestures.

Dithyrambic: they were also hot-blooded, yet that's where I reconditioned The Effectual Femme Fatale of Introspective Lore, to please help me find my way home, or start digging my grave now.

Pausing, when he felt like time was standing still, and the infantile ghosts returned as a collage of his own morbidity; to retrieve the private sector of his own introspective soul; time-honored, time-consumed.

Audaciously, I groveled, begging for the femme fatale to reset my legs; or give me a new pair of walking sticks, as well as a new integument. Humanely, that's where the seamstress of an old wives' tale reattached both of my appendages, by the earthlier flowerbeds of a much more tranquil place called Ataraxia, replacing all of my cuticles with a much more flowery image of a toddler's beginnings, providing me with a much more colorful layer of skin.

As a result, curling the goose bumps of the florists that were also grinning with the grimmest yards of bark, lawn, even plants, but eye-catching to the whole body of knowledge: For them that was botanical lore, for me it was just trying to cross the highway of morbidity; respectfully, in regards to the scientific notations, as well as the scientific timetables of my own epidermis. Deliriously excited, I was grateful, theurgically, and respectively.

Stems

Acclaimed: that's where I fell asleep and woke up by the thaumaturgical invocation of telesthesia, where I was able to stop grimacing and take baby steps by some miracle of irreality; without a diaper, and without a binky, without a walker, and without a jar of baby food. I was now the spitting image of a real man with a much more, deeper understanding of real men; as it pertained to introspection.

I called it the Stems of My Internalized Introspection, the stems of my hocus-pocus, allowing me to walk again, favorably, if not safely. So that I wouldn't fall over again, looking for the time-aged stampedes of manhood while rummaging through the earth's landscape. And then I found them; amidst the mist, and amidst the most remote corners of the world. Without being stepped on, and without being persuaded otherwise, even if it did cost me my life.

Parapsychologically, it was worth the journey. By now my intellect and self-awareness were also bleeding profusely; but it was stanch, and I was recompensed, healed by the psychic apparatus of conceit. That was the requital, that was the reward, the one I called GUERDON, educating me on the road to redemption, and the road to psychic readings with the greatest importance.

That's when I knew that I had a real purpose in life. Attributed, that was the moment of self-enlightenment. THE REVELATION, the one that I could not forget. Giving up, that's when I also wanted to quit the race, right there and then, knowing that I was not fulfilling the obligations, or the requiem (the Mass, celebrated for the repose of the souls of the dead), *including my own or the requirements that would lead me into the good graces of heaven.*

Yet I was convinced otherwise by the powers of persuasion, to distinguish myself from the mediations of life and death, as well as the things that I could still control; moderately, if not relatively.

Speaking privately by the bell of the church tower: down below the monks and nuns were also retreating to their monasteries, secluded under the roofs of their religious vows; while the mice and rodents created more of a fuss. The uproar: a bedtime hullabaloo.

Rhetorically speaking with the capacity to endure, I had more persistence, becoming more and more clear about the meanings of words. How it was all combined, as well as the expressions and styles of death: how it was all fractured; by, through, and with the faces of personalities.

Proud, like the spirits of the eagles that were also flying, to and from the otherworldly domains, transporting drinking water from the oceans below, to the hyperboles of the clouds that also adapted and found a new way to live; when the surface of the earth became too uninhabitable for humanity; we, they, and them. All of us, everybody, and everything that ever called the surface of the earth home.

Prefaced, that was their own conclusion, and that was their own conjectural speculation, not my own; slaying the faith of one-thousand-year old elm trees that were also dying, at risk of being overthrown by the earth's history, with a myriad of distressful feelings, losing their own faith in humanity, more importantly, losing their age-old rings.

Hypothesizing, that was the future, and this was our planet. Realistically, as time goes on, from the effects of climate change, and the effects of earthly metamorphosis.

Clued in, I was much more informed about the criteria of life. So I kept on pedaling with an odor of elegance, as well as more feelings of superiority.

Arrogantly, that was the spinal cord of my self-confidence, as well as the synthesis of my own sclerosis; tenacity; combining and completing the constituent elements of life and death as they continued to evolve; slowly, but circular, and eventually.

Abnormally, I was overwhelmed, in a roundabout way; mired and soiled by ten years of introspection. Sequentially; deprecating to the faith-

less soul; but mine still had faith, and it always would, unduly damaging the synthetic tissue of my own convictions; for good or for bad, just not my beliefs.

Tick, tock, tick, tock.

That was the sound of the carnage that I left contorting involuntarily; stripped of their lungs, dislodging the tenure of my own tenure. Screaming, unyieldingly, from the pivotal moments of my disconcert, to the pivotal moments when I suffered the unfair ruffles of a lifelong dream, waning away; recolored with shades of morbidity that I shared, quietly with the ghostly colors of wan.

Brazen, brazen, not so brazen—at least not anymore.

Supple, remorse could never have been so disarranged; confusion and upheaval could never have been so limber. Bending backwards; I began to free-fall into the depths of my own abysmal lither; at a rate and velocity that no other man or woman could ever comprehend; much less survive. Scrambling, I began searching for an implacable soul amongst the cluster of critters; entering the mode of survival.

Brazen, brazen—much more brazen: talkative, but never unavailing, or especially futile.

Ebullient: *I was a few miles away from heaven or hell, nothing in between, except for the light of my angelic visualization. To triumph or not to triumph; that was the question that I asked myself, when I was hovering on the clouds of the eminent, spiritual encounter.*

Thinning, the oxygen was a scarce, underestimated amenity of life; pale, faint, deficient of color. Onward; Brazen Maven was crazed; but his spirit resumed in his voyage with silent valor; highlighting the imposing signs of introspective cozen. Coveted; despite the self-deceit, trickery; as well as harder feelings of shame, even harder feelings of emotion that brought them all together; evaporating, rapidly.

Breathing heavily, he had more trouble breathing. Panting badly. Those were the whelps of the echoes, as well as the whelps of euphemisms. Those were the black and blue colors of his own exhilaration, just as much as his sacrifice to the world.

Bloodied, in dire straits, critically injured with a few torn anthers; enraged, he was still pallid, but not yet buried. Furious; he was rigid, but made of resolute. Evolving, with unyielding determination; that was the circuit, as well as the circle of self-introspection.

Straightforward, will-o'-the-wisp' despite the laceration of his will; that was a shared characteristic of introspective men. Upon nightfall, the moon turned the color of death, felt with beams of permanent cessation, struck by pebbles of reality that were also floating in outer space.

Veritably, sincerity was also settling in; but not before he was gravely ill, deathly, if not ghostly; only answering to the volatility of the compelling subversion; reengaging in the journey of a lifetime with a newly found perspective.

Unrivalled, he found himself riding alone. That was the common theme of autonomy, as well as introspection, pondering, wondering, about the hourglass of a grandfather clock that was inverted, running out long before he was ever supposed to die.

Said of Seize, as well as Seizure

Hemorrhaging, he found himself paralyzed by the front doors of extinction, enthralled by the vestige of his own death; notoriously, day after day. He thought about the struggles of less fortunate men than he ever was; and how he was blessed with the loveliest rose petals of respiration; barely. In church, he thought about his own sins for which he had not fully atoned, but he knows that he will one day, in the end, before he enters the confessional for the very last time.

Compartmentalizing Himself

From the annuals and the perennials that had already completed their life's cycles; perishing back into the earth's biosphere, to the biennials that will never be born again; arriving, he traveled a long distance. For ten long and drawn out years he invested in a journey that would submerge him into the kingdom of his noteworthy demise.

That was his tour of the world, from here to there. That was his view of the ecology; from the clouds, to the vault of heaven, or the basement of hell, as long as sovereignty was somewhere nearby.

Hallelujah, hallelujah, hallelujah.

Chapter 14

Prosopopoeia

A figure of speech in which an imaginary, absent, or deceased person is represented as speaking or acting.

Prosopopoeia: that was the plaint; said of funeral songs, as well as his own personal lamentation.

Educed and evoked; more notably, he was disappointed in himself, for not finishing what he originally started. *Resilient* that was another slogan of introspective men (his in particular). Tomorrow it might be something else, magnetized and saturated by the same science of rain showers that were also dousing his spirit with a rainfall of perceptive retrospection.

Vexed, his oversights were elicited, interwoven with wreaths of great emancipation; liberating, freeing him, uprooting him from the stranglehold of such strategic horticulturists, as well as the flowery gardens with their own brand of nursery rhymes.

Gratefully, he was spared by the ghosts of primitive human beings. Comparatively; the finish line was arrogated (claimed, unwarrantably and presumptuously, ascribed and appropriated to the individual); the one that mattered the most in life; drawing nearer and nearer to the chain links that were also supported by the greatest advocates of morbidity. That was the suicidal ideation of the devil, and only the wrath of God could timely destroy.

All-powerful: those were the fruits of his labor; bewildered by the imputations of his own resistance, feeding the breeding ground for more deceptions; of the truth, as well as lies; said of introspection, as well as morbidity, said of sovereignty as well as the eternal imprisonment of metamorphosis.

Hooray, hooray—those that remained in the crowd cheered, for the resolution of the great endeavor; glowing with divisive perceptions of an accounted heaven, just as much as divisive perceptions of an unaccounted functionality. That was hell, that was his life, from day one, through the rose petals of time.

Jolted, the shock waves reverberated; furtively, and quantitatively. Stone-faced, the rest of the infantile ghosts were also expressionless. Those that were greatly abhorred regressed back into their otherworldly time capsules. Evanescing; surreptitiously.

Politely the crowd subsided and the infantile ghost returned for one last hurrah; terminating, decoding the ensemble of Brazen Maven's discontent. Rendering; he unleashed the consonant voice of bewail and hurtfulness. For whom the power of life and death would timely destroy. That was the inharmonious plumage of the *Phylum chordata*, plucked away from the backs of the most innocent birds.

Miraculously, he felt the sensation of human emotion again for a split second in time; just before expiring back into the infinity of the plausible or implausible macrocosm; extinguishing and quelling the flame for the inconsonant duration of sensationalism and realism; making him the bedsheet whistler of after-death ghosts.

And then he was gone, returning to the woe of many years ago, when he was razzed and razed by the razor blades of the most biased radicals that slit his throat when he was just a ten-year-old little boy, meeting the finer details of the devil in person by the boiling coves of The Twin River of Echoes.

Incontinent; he was killed by the nature of penitence for urinating on the most endearing colors of life. Those were the flowers, primarily the roses; killed off by the nature of the radicals that were also ostracized from the flowerbeds and botanical gardens of the earth.

That was the nature of the rose petals (with a voice of their own) that did not condone the acts or inhumane acts of demonology. That was the hand, as well as the act of The Infernal Mortal Retriever, who sent him six feet below the earth's surface.

Whistling, whipping, and bustling: All things considered, those were the sounds of the fiercest winds; angrily, and dismally with a celebration of life in the realm of unsynchronized societies.

Said of Brazen Maven: far beyond the immeasurable chronometers of obsequiousness. Piercing the clammy spores of his skin, tortured by the feathers of the scandalous agenda.

Unscrupulous, for miles, and miles, and miles of self-introspection. Then he expounded upon the inner-makings of his odyssey; marking the deadline of his own chicanery with a shortness of sympathy, as well as a shortness of miracles; unearthing the epic astuteness of metamorphosis.

Lengthened, his life had been extended by the second hand of dutiful conundrums; reconnecting himself with his morals, from here to the grassy hills of eternity. Submitting and admitting; full heartedly, re-identifying himself with the word *eidolic* (defined as something or someone that is ideal or perfect, something that doesn't even exist).

Up until this point, that was sovereignty. Corpselike, he was shackled by the face of endeavor; foaming from the mouth. By now delirium prose was well-established, surpassing the bottommost conditions of the widespread desperation; a failure of unspeakable proportions. He had not fulfilled his obligations; to himself, or to the Lord.

Said of the spirit, as well as the soul: terminally ill.

Blinking for every subordinate ghost that disappeared, there was an equal and preeminent ghost that reappeared; apparitional, cadaverous, insomuch as wraithlike. Preparing himself for the end of a lifelong dream, he un-tucked his shirt and exposed the truth to the idiocy of his own falsity.

Grandstanding on Center Stage: The Podium of the Hypothetical Panache

Unshackled; that's when my spirit finally went back to spill my guts. Windblown, the same place where I saw the sickly image of myself dying with a visceral image of my own faults and failures, as well as a vomitus portrayal of my own morbidity that was splattered with deeply entrenched rubble from the great collide. For me that was abstractionism, causing the fuzzy hairs and problems of the world to explode.

Realistically, that's when I also spilled my facts, circumvented by the convenience of lies; for which I was positively convinced; initially, but then I matured. Surprisingly; my dignity was still swept away by the brooms of colorless servants.

Distanced from the seeds of reality: *sidetracked at the end of my adventure I encountered a four-hundred-year-old pirate that was intercalated from the century of presumption and distasteful assumption.*

Distressfully, he cried, and cried, and cried: Boo-hoo hoo; he also had his feelings hurt by the mean words of children during my quest for sovereignty. Anyway, anyhow; and by any means necessary; he was also offensive, like all hornswoggles of the world naturally are, and he was hoarse, satiric with an arthritic repulsion, as well as a fragile assurance of himself. That's when I thought I was going to hell, as a breach of etiquette, unnecessarily.

Heartbroken, he was born after the stygian cradle of humanity; also known as the compassionate pirate of the mimicking seas. Humorously, claiming to have witnessed the death of civility. When men cursed at women, and no longer opened their doors. That was the great descent of all gentlemen who have ever lived on this place called earth. Jocosely; but then he claimed to have witnessed the birth of incivility; solemnly, cataloguing his own age, as well as his own believability.

Coincidentally, that was the same geologic period of time. Jesting, when civility was valued at nothing more than a unit of sterling worth, and he was nothing more than a barbed, irritating drunk; atypical behavior from the strings of immoral puppetry.

Astringent: he was harshly biting; metamorphosing himself into a bicycle that put Brazen Maven on his back and carried the weight of his morbidity for ten consecutive years of unmatched, but qualified introspection.

Disclosed, he was the most preposterous droll of the drolls. Unconfined—gnawed, chewed and comically gnarled by the waggish tails of quizzicality.

Tolerant or intolerant, he was also the most measureless, and the most inestimable frontiersman of the acerbic mongers that built their own amphitheaters, for the entertainment of their audiences with a historical acumen.

Exceedingly caustic, he was bitterly pungent: tawdry, selfish with the framework of nonsensical pirates from the genealogy of the jocular seas, an infamous bastard of lunacy with an untraditional constitution; improvising his own way through the asylums of time and space with a horde of acrid remarks, as well as an incomplete perceptivity of his own factuality, or even the droves of fatality.

Impoverished: all good bicycles break down in life, just like all good old fashioned pirates are destined to consign themselves to the worms of morbidity. Feasting on their own hilarity, they were the only ones that made themselves laugh while wearing the grins of coaxing swindlers, likened to the countenance of suspicious constituents.

Derisive, he wore the personality of a repulsive, stinky swashbuckler; farting, beeping his horn on the most exquisite flowers of life (including my own); making them all wilt and rescind their colors of beatitude (including my own), as well as their colors of indisputable rectitude (including my own).

Mirthfully: his family tree began subsiding with a foul and equal quality about the relativity of its own history.

Har-har. Moreover, that was a fine example of the pirate's vulgarity; depreciating the collectivity of his own wheels (snide, but he was always by Brazen Maven's side; that was his mode of transportation), as well as the collectivity of his own morals that were survived by the keenly distressing feelings of an overwrought civilization, for which he could not endorse as a meritorious virtue; unless it pertained to him; jovially.

Brazen Maven: Much More Realistic

In the garden of truth, he was protected from the rain itself, as well as the sun, and all of its glory; elaborating on his own motives under the awnings; using the velariums for his own personal use; that was the platform of restless hallucination.

Self-patronizing. *As a personal assessment, I was incensed by the furnace of dissimilitude; where I was initially frozen, but then I was unthawed. Eventually, I was steamed again, glazed, and nearly baked to death, which I found unacceptable as it pertained to me. Impulsively; I was heavily diluted, disoriented by the craftsmanship of the fanatical fireplace.*

I was, I was, levitating on the verge of sovereignty, flirting with the curious nature of euphemisms. Ultimately, fulfilling my own personal obligations, not only to myself, but more importantly to the Lord because I was forever his, and he would be forever mine.

Discombobulated: Coming Home

For the longest time I was incarnate, out of touch with reality, and for the longest period of time I was trying to figure out the purpose of my own existence; fleshly or un-fleshly. Those were the complications of my heart, as well as the complications of my mind, complicating matters even more, my whole life had been clouded by the clouds of beetles, and the larvae that liked to feed on the dung, as well as the fungus, and the rest of the plant parts.

Dressed in black attire, that's when I attended a funeral with the biting gnats (a.k.a. those were the punkies), *and the rest of the black flies, for the finalization of my own metaphorical accounts, as well as the original image of my own bountiful harvest, highlighted by the sunset of my life, when the most beautiful angels in the history of the world greeted me with a kiss, and whispered sweet nothing's into my ears.*

Those were my reminders daily: those were the colors of my rainbows, as well as their own resolution of black and white. In the final period of our lives, they were also not the finest hours of my own realiza-

tion; but the worst, in regards to the compost, as well as comparison and contrast.

Preset by the hour hands of beginnings and conclusions. That was the Ditto, Ditto, Reiterated factor, reincarnated by the roots of the plant life that never really died, in synchronization with the loveliest rose petals, akin to the perception of the prettiest little girl that I ever encountered. From love at first sight, until death do us part, and it finally did; fatefully.

For the longest period of time (as it pertained to my life), I could never figure it all out by myself, until my feminine, angelic visualization reappeared to me near the homonyms of The Twin River of Echoes, with the most heavenly voice that led me to believe…she was, she was, the same little girl that I first fell in love with many years ago, when I was just a sweet little boy that would one day redecorate the living rooms of hell with his own brand of metamorphosis.

But that was yesteryear. When I was just a wee bit, little plant of the earth, trying to figure out the laurels of time and space, likening me to the metaphorical morsels that were also written about in forbidden novels.

Love never dies, and for me it never did, it lived on—transferred, renowned, retransformed with colors of my own history that will eventually determine my own spiritual crown, growth, even fate; by, through, and with my own otherworldly energy.

"I love you, with the fondest memories," she said to me.

That was the fleshly incarnation of the human body that brought us back together, but that was also the same fleshly incarnation that drove us apart. That was the great wedge that neither of us could ever overcome. That's what I believed then, and it's what I believe now.

Revolving, that was the revolutionary cycle of the flowers. Those were the roses primarily. Blindly, but that was the best thing that ever happened to me. I just don't know it then, but I know it now, lacking life's full experiences, like I had never experienced it before.

And so we met again. Ironically, that was the full cycle of Ditto, Ditto, Reiterated. I loved her more than my life itself. Her spirit, ever-restless; just like my own, and I never really knew that she died, nor did I know if she was consumed by the beetles or the larvae. Those were the predators of the world's most beautiful flowers. Yet from that day forward

I always wondered what my life would've been like if I had not been so preoccupied by my own search for sovereignty.

Rewriting history: that was the impossible feat of selection, as well as the impossible feat of introspective men; incarnate or discarnate, yet it was still the dream that I could always dream about, and it was always the wish that I could always wish for, understanding that it could never be anything more or anything less.

Regrettably, I wish that we both could've lived and died in the same flowerbeds of the earth's botanical gardens; with a much more positive outlook; as it pertained to the love of my life. Not necessarily for ourselves but for the future, as well as the grandchildren of Mother Nature. She was the matriarch of the earth's habitation; my figurative mother, as opposed to the morbid background that blackened the curious nature of euphemisms.

In regards to Mother Nature—*culpable: that was my fault, my morbidity, and I alone was to blame. Remorseful, for not being able to change the things in life that I could not change. That was the past, and this is the present, where the future has come upon me. My time is now; the end of the world is coming, I just can't change it.*

Recultivating memories: she provided me with the answer to my own quest for sovereignty. Enlightening me, helping me lay the foundation for the last chapter of my life.

Lovingly, that was Mother Nature when I was moaning, partially sovereign, but still groaning, from the thorns of my own past, to the thorn-less pastures of my own future.

Repining: I was ranting and raving, pondering the long road home by The Twin River of Echoes, having to say goodbye. I just wasn't in a hurry. Time will never end. I'm sure heaven can wait, just a few days more.

Heartfelt, when I eliminated the perception of Gadfly, The Lore of Extrospection from my life, my heart began to throb. Immediately I was elated from so many years of adverse effects, squandered opportunities that would never be extended to me again. Nor could I ever afford them. I was broke, introspectively as well as hopefully, cracked and cleaved, morbidly.

Disjunctive, those were the injuries I sustained, slowly murdering my will to live. Those were the episodes of my own instability, the constant drama of my life, even in my dreams, killed off by the steam from the well springs that I could not seem to stabilize.

Bewailing; that was the nature of morbidity; furious in its natural state; more glorious from the relics, or the replicas of the dead human beings that were also resting, somewhere else, in the heavenly beds of the great beyond.

In summation, Gadfly was the worst of all, more so than all the others combined, an imagined creature of the earth that lived amongst us, and I could not persuade otherwise to rewrite the story of his own life that precluded me.

United, we were all divided by death. I guess that's the way it was supposed to be, even for me, but somehow I still felt a special connection to him, a unique companionship that not even the bees could remanufacture in their bee hives; fracturing my inner-spirit with a series of detrimental lies, creating more detrimental effects; not only to myself, but to everyone else as well.

Tart: interesting and provocative, but always piquant, no matter what it was; as a reference point, that was the foundation of my own conformed cognition, transcended by the laurels of supernatural divinity, where anything and everything in life was made more plausible through the process of metamorphosis.

Discredited by the standing ovations of the methodical profiles in the crowd that refused to go away; all of which were propagating; regenerating at an alarming rate; stunningly, they were all neglected at first, but then they were resolved, firmly fixed, absolute; in their presence, as well as their manners; initially concealed by the absurd adumbrations that carried an indispensable requisite.

Thinking back to all of his glory, he had a knack for the contrived; and an even bigger knack for the unimaginable, broadening the parameters of his own otherworldly horizons. Departing, his spirit turned the color of a black, foreshadowing tome. Behold, that was the unheeded obituary of his exceeding life.

Vincit Omnia Veritas

Truth conquers all. In remembrance, of the truth, and everything but the truth.

Then he was alleviated from the weight of the world, and the
weight of the universe. His spirit was whisked away; at last, at last
dragging his feet, as well as his name by the phantasmal ghosts of
yesteryear, reflecting upon the degradations of yesterday so that his
ghostly relics could finally begin to wither away; and then erode into
the universal trench with a vague and blank configuration.

Self-defining, those were the whispers of the plants that were
also embattled by the whispers of transparency. Giving in, he yielded
to the sounds of the spectrals that were hiding in the background
with a customary arrangement of flowers, candles, even urns; inviting the yellow-bellied marmots that were also living and dying in the
same widespread realm as the introspective bicyclist.

Writhing, that was the pain of his memories; naturally. So was
the pain of his breathlessness, when he stopped breathing and died
abruptly, endlessly, but not unequivocally. Suspended; his mind continued to live on, as a travesty of his own preternatural existence.

Hesitating, he still had to crossover, but the time was near, just
not now. Regardless; it was coming, sooner; rather than later. Still
ranting. Yes, indeed. Year ten was the year of the tedious whirlwind,
when his spirit danced his way onto the threshold of the interpretive
daunting, slow dancing his way into the arms of the sovereign phase.

Long and hard, scripted or unscripted, that's where he also
forged the subculture of his own death, converging on the pinnacle of
the defiling chastity; desecrating to the soul; harrowing. Whimsically,
he was still connected to the same timberlines of his own discontin-
uance: impure, tainted, egregiously violating.

Punctuated, he capitalized and reestablished his own crop of
gametes; unchaste; but that was the pollution of the tormented spirit.
Convulsive; he began having more trouble recapturing the oddities
of his own remoteness, joined by the throng of strong negativity that
was linked to the guidelines of abstractionism.

From the farthest and endmost to the ceremonial use of his own immediacy, spotless in the ripples of the laundered, instigating rivulet; gory in the bloodstained outlets of reality, where he could never have met or encountered the spirit of The Mourning Echo.

Deciphered, she was the little girl that petted and caressed him when he was just a little, unassuming creature of the earth, before she met the leaves, and the currents, as well as the ripples of the earth's cruelty that would symbolize the ethos of her own fate by The Twin River of Echoes.

For now and forevermore, he was also botched by the tombstones that were projecting unwritten etiquette rules; interpreted by the matriarchal dowager of wistfulness, woven with substances of hidden insinuation.

Said of dysphoria: he was downcast, unlike anything else the world had ever seen before. Enumerative, he recalled there was an impulsive tombstone, dedicated and inscribed especially for him, with a feeling of disconsolation, as well as a feeling that no other word or phrase could ever begin to describe.

Required: for the particular purpose: *Here lies the ascertained symbol of metamorphosis: desolate, tristfully, low-spirited, morbidly, but not completely dissatisfied.*

More Raving

Hence, that was the tombstone, when he defied the odds and lived a partial life, just not the right or intended life that a metaphorical flower of the earth was meant to live.

Duped and more poignantly, he was ashamed, of himself, as well as humanity: As a preliminary action to the broader scope with a higher importance level.

Those were the words preceding his real name—*Svelte* engraved with chisels into the slabs of graphic rock. Unruffled, he was ten thousand rose petals removed from the comparative forms of innocence, as well as the comparative forms of delicacy, withdrawn and demoralized by stoic memories of his own childhood, extracted from the wreck and ruin of the blood-riddled puzzles when he was just a poor little boy of the happy-go-lucky planet that was trying to make his way in the gender bias, prejudice world.

Esteemed or unesteemed so that he could not feel, sense, or touch the intangible things in life. Researching; furthermore, it was all true to life, pieces of reality that were denied, especially for him; cruel, crude, even rude, but not necessarily definitive, or explicative.

Disillusioned: those were the secrets, as well as the deceptions, involving the delusions that were all unveiled by the guardians, as well as the sabotage of the beastly plight with an intractable occurrence; attributed to the touchstones of his own poetic fondness. From the safe keepers of his grave, to the safe keepers of his grace land that had an uncanny eeriness about it; improving the fluidity of the rills. That was the full disclosure of his obscurity; serene, but still encompassed; by, through, and with a marvelous quality about it.

Frowning; noting or referring to the mood; he was dejected, drooping, crestfallen. Horridly; he was characterized by the same atomic phenomena of modality, treachery, as well as a branch of inarticulate faithlessness, uttered and re-uttered with a cloth of unreliable readiness.

Said of the spirit, from the elevated laws of superfluous gravity: Humbled by the computation of answerability. Reliving the letters of abscission; falling, expeditiously, and lugubriously; relieving himself from the burden of his own burden; or the obligation of his own obligation.

Hastily, either way, his spirit collapsed from the insecure, unstable, articulation of the clouds. That was The Hypothetical Castle in The Sky, where all of the introspective flowers once resided in the company of speculation and hyperbole; flowering the earth, narrated, by, through, and with the false footings of the clouds, as well as the false sense of his own security.

Carefully calculated: those were the equations of life that finally began to make sense, unambiguously. Consciously or unconsciously, he was reminded that he died in the haphazard mile of the great race; revealing the conception of the truth.

Excruciatingly, his spirit was elongated by the discourse of unscripted epithets, but that was the elation of the ghosts. That was the perception of life and death: Chronicled long before he was ever stereotyped as the editor of his own redaction, so that his soul could finally rest in peace.

Whistling into the saintly hospitality of his own tractability. Long before he was ever crowned the victor of the most intimate race; and long before there was a resolution of his own restlessness. For him that was the moment of closure, overcome with a pyramid of feelings, as well as a pyramid of schemes and emotions that drove everyone else apart halfheartedly.

Propitiously, he prevailed over the history of his own dominant shadows, succeeded by the ultimate wake, defined and understood in the analogues of malignant diaries.

In solidarity, there was an aggregation; the mass, a large collection of benign, omnifarious ghosts that were conjoined, gathering together, reappearing to help escort him back to the more traditional home of the dead; heart-rending; of or relating to the more conventional cradle of humanity; altruistically.

Excessively, he was blinded by the glares of the expletives, overshadowed by the group of cavernous trolls that were swearing at him, cursing, trolling his spirit from the ridge of the crummiest crag. Those were the casualties that he left in his wake, preventing him from entering the rigor mortise stage of death.

Looking back on his own chronological notations with baseless loathing; that's when he reinterpreted the meaning of life with a more terminable message: unmodified.

Ashes to Ashes: The Elegy

Congé (a leave-taking; the great farewell; a sudden dismissal); *these are the final hours of my life. From the depths of the infinite well I was projected, to the flowery beds of my own imagery; where I shall return, one day, with a host of new friends, and a smaller cast of old ones, as well as the same memories that will keep me company in the fragrant*

THE SOVEREIGN ROSE OF MORBID LORE

gardens of the afterlife. That is heaven; with a small amount of enemies that will also make me question the validity of my own existence.

Put forth, from the hands of mankind; bloodied, stitched, with makeshift stitches; quails that were used from the backs of dissected porcupines. That was life as I knew it when I was still living, but it was nothing compared to the most beautiful place of all that was still waiting for my spirit to arrive, with an open invitation to sit at the dinner table as the chairman of sovereign dinners in heaven.

Silencing the words, even the sounds of the firestorms, as well as every other sound of morbidity: *Which I wouldn't trade, even if I had to die, all over again, as a human being, each and every day until the end of time; as long as I knew that heaven would be my final resting place, just on the other side of darkness.*

Chapter 15

Dying, the Rose: Said of Morbidity
The Dirge, Said of Reflection,
as well as Memorable Happenstance

I *remember the earth fondly: Chapfallen, in remembrance, voices of the dead; speaking despondently, from beyond the grave; in the third person. That's how I have chosen to share my past with the eardrums of the earth. These are my memories that I would like to elucidate, with all of my watery eyes, as witnessed by the umbrellas of father time, and all of his creation.*

My threnody; when I died, my only request, and my only wish was, that I be buried next to the bee hives; so that I could hear the buzzing of the bees; unchangingly.

Buzz, buzz: Bringing me vibes of inner-peace and tranquility: Right next to the drunken moderator of The Twin River of Echoes; *so that I could feel the pain of his indifference; continuously. Now that I have fulfilled my end of the bargain, the rest is up to him.*

Asunder, Svelte's spirit was thrust violently, split up and torn into separate parts and pieces, tossed and revolved into the never-ending cycle of time and space. Set forth; where anything and everyone in life that was specialized by the subplot of a tragic finale was also corrupted, but not distressed by the cycle of life itself.

Unperturbed and not so deeply regrettable; his spirit was no longer pending, but greatly enriched by the bountiful cycles of life and death, as well as the bountiful cycles of never-ending morbidity that came along with metamorphosis.

Speaking from the scripture of a tired, stiffening soul, his spirit stopped levitating in the limbo of the purgatory; freely and openly without further expedience, or consequence, interruption, as well as pang.

Thoughtfully, I could not look back that far in time and be a better man for it, nor could I be a better flower because of it. Yet I was advantageous throughout the last decade of my own personal reflections. So I can still be optimistic and hold out hope that humanity will transcend itself from the dumpsters of foolish propaganda, turning itself into a more viable world without war; making me a seamless flower that carved its own niche in the grand scheme of emancipated wreaths.

Shamefaced, I was the morbid flower of the world that would likely be remembered in botanical history as the pioneer of self-introspection, with a morbid analysis; of my own history as well as the earth. Sorrowful, least I say, condemnatory.

Svelte: much more adventitious, self-effacing; these were the graphic details of his contrition.

Additionally, my virtuous humility died every day. Ironically, precluded by a lifetime of endless pursuit. Needful and needlessly, I was excluded by the laws of reality.

Unbecoming, I was not able to achieve the unattainable dream of the living while I was still living, but that was the crux of my expressive malady. Even so, I still managed to avoid the diabolical trails that disfigured the wanting of my own perdition.

Dismantling, reconfiguring, and sulking over the molecular biology that would've killed me prematurely anyways. Subsequently, I followed the remaining bees that led me to the botanical carpets of heaven; where we were all fumigated by the inflorescence of the Promised Land.

Somehow, someway; that made me much more becoming; as a morbid flower of the earth, as well as a metaphorical plant of the universe that was also repulsed and disgusted by the memories of an untraditional fireside recount.

Those were my fireside stories.

Despite all of this, and all of that, I was still judged, convicted, and sentenced to an immutable, demoniacal, underworld incarceration, when I was scared of the devil, and I began running for my life, down the back stairs of hell, ruminating amongst the skulls and bones.

Discombobulated, even throughout the empyrean enchantment of his own utopia.

Griping, that's where I felt the most woes in life. That's where I felt the most throes in my route to death. From the maggots, to the bugs, from the clouds, all the way to Gadfly, The Lore of Extrospection, and all of his humanistic afflictions; grieving, grueling, life-stopping. So I stopped to pray, and the Lord answered my prayers. That's when I knew that I was loved by the creator of human kind. I am his child after all. Imperfect, but still his child nonetheless.

Animosity budded; subito, much like the pesticide venue with a musical direction from the depressive pianist by The Twin River of Echoes, drinking his life away; and not half as contrite as I was, confusing, but always objectionable.

Essentially, I was saved by the angelic visualization in the year that I was prevented from being eradicated from the earth altogether; into the vast and varied space of timeless enmities, or so I thought.

Perplexed, I just didn't know it until I was revitalized by the guardians of my own sensitivities. All of which were frail, susceptible, greatly perpetrated by the great wall of abstractionism.

As for the highlands themselves, they were all too lofty, difficult, arduous for me to climb; much less understand the full meaning of their existence, as it pertained to the anomalies of my own artistry, as well as the first responders of my own sensibilities.

Beheld: that was the solace that I took away from the visuals of my ironic affair; dreadfully. Insolvent, eventually I was brokenhearted; feeling sorry for myself, as well as the nature of pity; selfishly.

Dispossessed, I was abandoned, by the human forms of the marl (what I called the earth itself), but not the bees; whom I loved with all of my heart and were nearly expatriated by the theology of supernatural critters.

Described: they were the hornets, related to the family of bees, turned to images of my own craziness; momentarily, until they returned, more insane than ever before. Assaulting the earth's habitation with a global invasion; unlike anything the world has ever seen.

Alone at Night

That's when the moon spoke to me (if you think you are lonely now, please trade me places so that you can find out the true meaning of loneliness). I have no company, just a vague visual of friendship. From here, until I can see no more.

Beastly, that was the nature of the attack, and I could not protect myself or anyone else from it; in regards to the compilation of the cabalistic infantrymen, with all of their staples; rewording the complete works of cannon fodder. Caught off guard, I was attacked by an army of fire ants in the earliest years of the great deviation, as well as the latter stages of my own supermundane condition.

Ferociously, they thought about taking on humanistic behavior and beheading me in the numinous gallows, for stealing their red wine and breadcrumbs. Thankfully, that wasn't an option. Marching, in a single file line; they carried a bottle of whisky and celebrated their own victories; in life as well as death, but especially war and battle.

Besotted and staggering from the all-night benders, all the way to the relative hilltops, as well as the federation of general terrorists that were stockpiling grenades and verbal codes, reinforced with a reserve of homicidal pesticides, as well as iambic pentameter that would've blown my mind away; inhabiting my home, crawling on me; and then deciphering my super-ordinary beginnings.

Cast aside, they once called me The Solace of My own Solace. Their leader; which I was not, nor would I ever be, but I was still the emblem of their unplowed morals. That was the lesson of my life, when my faith never left me, even in my darkest hours, when I should've died, long before I actually did.

Buzz, buzz. *Truthfully, recovering from compression was never easy. I just made it more difficult than it ever had to be, but that was the resilience of the platonic spirit.*

Godly or ungodly, I still managed to rebound; somehow, someway; unspecified through buoyant sprigs of germination that were commonly associated with my botanical heritage.

Reformulated, that was the season of new beginnings, replacing the season of old habits, and a new ascertainment for life, but for me it was also the transitional phase of my own conversion: Said of praise and of praise alone; that was the transitional stage of my own exaltation; to the glory of heaven, for example.

Mindfully, those were the trials and tribulations of my own residential morbidity. I called it—Acknowledging the Receipts of My Own Self-Possessions. Costly, but it was worth the price. Yet for me it was death, the very same price that I would pay all over again.

Carefully crafted, I remember being weather-beaten from so many years of self-introspection; hideously. Unmasking the colors of filth and misery; combined, they still formed an accurate depicture of my own portrayal; picturesque, but still clouded by the cloudless computations of life and death, as well as the quixotic raindrops that fell from the greatest heights of heaven, just as much as the gases of the earth's perplexity.

Ill-boding; that's when the definition of squalor helped diminish my otherworldly possessions, primarily intellect, as well as the properties of self-awareness. Misunderstood, I was confused by the misapplied adjectives that helped describe me, derived from the cellars of my own personal designation; intimate and personally humbling. Those were the conjunct adverbs; as well as the plurals and adverbs; grievously, and profanely.

Corresponding, with the nouns, as well as the regular verbs, including the vibes of the sinister reality, recognizing the musical obfuscation of the toper pianist; he was the permanent fixture by The Twin River of Echoes that would seemingly never go away.

Baleful and always foreboding. I have not heard the last of that guy, even by, through, and with the conditions of death; there is so much more to be told about the story of his story, and the tale of his yarn that remains untold.

He has done something wrong that goes far beyond anything I can ever imagine. I can feel it in the air. I can even smell it on his breadth. I can sense it in the ambiance. I can see it in his bloodshot eyes. I can only hope that he hasn't let humanity down. If he has, then his soul will have to pay the ultimate price, in perpetuation. Until, if, and when God finally decides to forgive him for his sins.

Autonomy: that was the loneliest number on earth. I could feel the weight of his guilt, wanting to confide in me even through my grave. Until several years ago, when the choice was no longer his, and I was foreordained to die, with or without him, just as much as he was foreordained to live, with or without me. Timely or untimely, we shall see each other again, one day, in the vibrant colors of heaven—hopefully.

Fainthearted, I was sharply berated by the voices of the inflicted ghosts, exposing them for what they really were, symptoms of my own morbidity.

Piacular (Reparatory): The Ulterior, the Final Atonement

Before I used to hurt, and hurt, and hurt, with a sad and broken heart. Now I decompose with the voids that have left my spirit empty-hearted; for the evolution of my self-respect; excluding the possibilities of my own saintliness, existing far beyond the material world. That's when I lost interest in what I was and what I stood for.

Wanted or unwanted, those were the angelic visualizations of my own rectitude that helped inspire me to finish what I could not originally finish by myself, and to rectify the floral beauty of my own tenure that went unnoticed by the most glorious gardeners in the history of heaven.

That was the recurring theme when I parlayed my own condolences to the other flowers of the world, as well as vindication from the same angelic visualization that once inspired me to reconfigure the waterless stems of my self-pity; pathetically, but beneficent to the introspective soul.

Wringing, I must admit it, I remember entering the confessional for the very last time in my life, and for the very last time in my life I also felt the dank seeds of my own physiology regrow themselves, blossoming, reestablishing their own lifelines. I called it—Purifying: The Cycle of My Own Deathly Hexagons, Poor me, Poor me.

Said of progeny: *They were my offspring, they were my children, irrevocably; if not radically, to develop and revolutionize themselves as the most majestic flowers the world has ever known. Those were the roses. Just as I have; introspectively, as well as psychologically, if not visually, physically, as well as morally.*

Certainly, it was my belief in myself that helped carry me to victory; self-confident, eternally. That was the foundation of my introspection: nothing more and nothing less. Touching a part of myself that I never knew existed inside of me, deservingly and fittingly.

Posthumously, his spirit was cast forth; nudged and pushed forward; shunted, to meet the procession of reclusive mourners that were also soldered with rifles of human emotion by the gravediggers of the dystopian cemetery.

Humbly, that was his life in review. All-inclusive; they were the beetles, and they were the flies. They were the bees, and they were the gnats. They were the serpents, and they were the rodents, accompanied by the birds, squirrels, and even the rabbits, plus the autochthonous skunks that were also bred from *The Terrain of Urine and Romanticized Lands.*

Supernal, they were the prayers, and they were the hymns. They were the songs, and they were the melodies; including the worms, ants, and even the other insects and animals of the world that loved the most exquisite flower of all. That was The Sovereign Rose of Morbid Lore.

Offshoot, they were the children of God and Mother Nature that came together to honor his weightlessness. All the way back to the undesirable cribs of his own grass roots; when Svelte was battered, badly morbid, watered down by the exclamations of his own witty banter.

Heavy-hearted: his mind was obese with fatty tissue, weighed down by the scales of subjectivity; muddled with commemorative pieces of calm and stillness; remorseful, in the company of regrettable ghosts.

And so the pitiful tales of my woebegone days are done and over with; never to be revisited again; expressing an overabundance of gratitude; healing; expressively.

Extensively, I was damaged goods; too old and too decrepit to mummify or try and restore, but not to preserve. My time had come; my time was over, even the weeks, months, and years before that, I always felt like I was dead in every way imaginable.

So my spirit has returned to say goodbye, for one last time, to my memories, as well as my heirlooms. To my opinions, as well as the facts, even the ones that I could not prove, but not before I made amends with myself, and not for the approval of the external hyperboles, but for the validation of my own existence, as well as the sanctity of my inner-spirit, where I could still hear the voices of the bees, buzzing in my ears.

Candidly, I was immensely weatherworn, brimming with water worn grains of age; unalterably, faithfully, and reverentially…into the abounding paradise of a much more glorified heaven than I could ever imagine; teeming with a great quantity of docility, prolific.

Transference: Crossing the Transcendent Timeline of Life and Death

That was the liminal line of demarcation, pertaining to contradictoriness, said of mortality, as well as immortality; self-explanatory in his own words.

Now I lay my spirit down to sleep in the pantheon of introspective lore; replenishing the nutriments of my own faith with subtle hints of closure. That was the culmination; floating in the span of the ethereal convention; discovering the violation of the creed was never really the violation of the creed, but a mere expenditure of my own life that had a heavenly perception about it; as well as a heavenly visual that I could not retain; up until now. I guess that's why they called it life. Conclusively; I was no longer recuperating from so many years of deprecation, or errors in judgment, as well as opaque introspection.

Looking back, with serene vines that were grown from the seeds of his own memory, stored by the One and the Only Father of Time;

treasured with threads of roses that were accompanied by masculine, feministic qualities of memoriam.

Appreciatively, I was blessed, for having met the ghosts, as well as the bees. They were the only ones that sang for me when I lost my voice and couldn't sing for myself anymore. Shamefully, they were also the only ones that cried for me when I couldn't cry for anyone but myself. Vibrant, they even played their fiddles for me, buzzing, when I couldn't buzz anymore, or make a cup of honey and tea for the elderly folk. More importantly; they also played the violins and showed me how to smile when I couldn't smile anymore.

Reflection and Relegation: Reflecting Upon My Own Misnomers

The complaint; regression, the art of foreign dialect, as it pertained to the mind-set of cultural indifference; imbued by feelings of guilt with a reiteration of retrogression.

Miraculously, I still found my inner light amid the subterranean darkness when there was no other light, my biggest regret was the process of metamorphosis, having been transformed into a human being was the worst possible thing that ever happened to me.

Introspectively speaking—when I didn't get to live my full life as a flower, I wasn't able to change the world for the betterment of society. Yet I still feel like I left a lasting impression on the world, one that every little girl will always remember me by. That was my legacy; that was my dream, the one that never really came to fruition, even though my life was extended for it, and because of it.

The Trope: Dispersed from the Vault of Heaven

Forthrightly, I would rather have lived and died in my natural state of botany with the rest of the world's flowers; never having to experience the atrocities of mankind; most of which were self-created, not inherent, but taught, practiced, learned; stenciling the modus operandi of thankless human beings that lived on planet earth, destroying its natural habitat, far beyond repair (as it pertained to climate change).

As a whole, I never believed that it was okay to judge other people by the color of their skin, or the color of their beliefs. The way self-conceit overrode the maltreatment of people as a generalization, but it was all inhumane. Yet, that was the atrocity that I first witnessed when I was just a little, obeisant metaphor of the world, frolicking on the heaven-sent topsoil.

Convivially, I was goaded by the deposits of dishonesty and treachery, sold and given away to the stylish, emotionless repositories. Emotionally charged, I followed the remaining pollen into the clouds with a greater outburst of fragrance, as well as a heavenly irony that rained upon me with an ounce of grace, perfume, as well as ten thousand pounds of un-amiss bliss.

The Disclosure: Once a Flower, Always a Flower

That was the natural transition of life and death, and I was not really an introspective man of the world, but just a decorous, obeisant flower that lived and died with a specialized inclination for sovereignty.

In hindsight, I lost my way when I was just an unassuming little flower. Yet I was still grand in my personal appearance. Those were the general effects of my stateliness; changeless, but still crystal clear, clearly-cut.

Faintly, those were the general effects of my majesty, as well as the leitmotif of my dignity; highly ambitious, idealistic; as proven by the motley bees.

Likable or unlikable, they never really bothered me or antagonized me. In fact, they kept following me, even when I was color blind, all the way to my first colors of death. Buzzing, they showed me the real colors of life when I couldn't see them for myself anymore. That's when I lost my eyes, and I was blinded by the possibility of spending eternity in hell.

Ever-present: I enjoyed their company, making me feel obliged. I will always remember them because they embraced me and loved me for who and what I really was unconditionally, regardless of my body language, foreign dialect; or especially the overtone of my creed.

Buzz, buzz—those were the only words they ever used. Buzz, buzz. But they were the only words they ever needed. With every buzzing sound there was a different connotation, a different lisp, a different intonation that was indescribable to human beings: Buzz, buzz—that was the language of the bees, far more intricate and expansive than the human language will ever be, basic in its concept, unworldly in its origin, as well as its destination.

Responsive; they lauded me. Buzz, buzz; they eulogized me with every laden buzzing; praising me, including me into their own personal lives with a bonnet, as well as a menology of friendship. Metaphorically; they were also an integral part of my own integrity, for which I never underscored, estimated, or especially discounted.

Wrought or unwrought; that was the story of my story; stupefied, unclear about my role in life; until I took on the form of an unmistakable man with an unmistakable substance. That was the process of metamorphosis, making me pedantic, an experienced expert of the world that was overly concerned about his own convoluted ideas, formulas, even formalism; maiming my remains with a blade of coil and foil, crippling me throughout the scatological effects of my own globe trekking.

Disparaged, I was born self-absorbed; from the rain, as well as the sun; highlighted by the ostentatious colors of the geysers with courage and frankness, as well as entitlement. For that I am truly sorry Lord, I have overstepped my bounds. Those were the stepping stones of retrograde, lesser organisms.

Please forgive me, God. Since I have sinned, I am still waiting in line, by the backyards of heaven. I apologize for stealing the breadcrumbs of the ants, as well as the feelings, stimulus, thoughts, and emotions of others, especially less fortunate flowers than I ever was, but I still feel comfort in the presumption that I am, and always will be incapable of hurting others in reality.

Uncoiled: that was the solace of my solace; unbelievably, when my vision was confirmed; by, through, and with the solidified assurance of my own reassurance, and that I was only meant to beautify the world; in aeternum; until I was taunted, harassed, intimidated by the imperilment of the imperative daunting; unavoidable, for me at least.

Gratuitously, I have been dead for several years now, thoroughly consummated, veritably; shedding the legend of my own metacognition, redecorating the colors of my own corrosion, as well as the colors of a brand new, sudden existence.

That was the great de facto: when I became more erosive. Genetically, that was deleterious to the introspective soul, but that was also a part of my own sacrifice to the world, as well as my parentage; that I speak of, and about; endearingly.

Synonymously, I was satisfied with the end result, but that's only because I never sought perfection, just happiness; which was the equivalence of sovereignty.

Summarizing: those were the common bonds of deathly flowerbeds and the common bonds of timelessness, with compounding deathbeds.

Shrouded, my corpse was wrapped for burial in a cloth that was fabricated; by, through, and with the amiability of the bouquets, denoted from the neighboring gardens of fraternal and sororal similarities.

Set to reproduce, they were the sequelized flowers, equalized and symbolized, colored and recolored by melancholic overtones. Yet they were all placid; next to the nectarines, pears, and even the plums of heaven's gardens.

Regardless, they were still engaging in the sacrificial landscape of my own terminal dawn. Uprooted; that's when nine hundred caterpillars turned into nine hundred doctrines of perseverance while I was still waiting for an interview with God at the doorsteps of heaven; filling the earthly air with a lovely touch from the receptacles of my own cultural phenomenon.

Dignified. *Éclat, from the palms of the divine I was erected, with a certain, brilliant resilience as it pertained to artistry. Reinforced, I also persevered with rose petals of intellectualized anecdotes; none of which were still blooming, but decomposing with thorns of verisimilitude, as well as thorns of irascibility.*

From whence I came, and to whence I shall return; derived from the same incendiary roots that once inspired me to become an introspec-

tive man of the world, with an introspective devotion to God, as the first and foremost authority of creation.

From the floral designers, to the boundless butterflies that were fluttering about, and to my own personal atrocities that I once committed, but could not go back in time and change, even though it was expected of me. Not from anyone else, but myself. That, and only that, is what I called self-respect.

Echoes, the reverberation. Once a metaphor, always a metaphor.

En fin. At the gateway of heaven I was worthy of God; ambrosial, when heaven asserted itself as the priority and could no longer wait for my personal quietude.

Free at last. I was uprooted from the earth's topsoil, once and for all by the way of God, or the hand of doom, I never really knew, and I never really cared. I just believed that I was exceptionally succulent, pleasing in taste, forgivable, aberrant in my personal smell.

Free at last from the stranglehold of metamorphosis. Now I was re-instilled, with a brand new, delicious fragrance of rapture. Edible, but still well-received by the heavenly perceptions of the greatest angels that ever lived; who knelt and prayed with me in the same braided gardens of life; painting a ten-year portrait of myself with the trademark colors of a hair-raising century. That was the incorrigible rave of my incorrigible fate; interminably.

The Quantum Leap

On my sanctified day of reckoning, I exited the earth as a remnant of its own memory that would one day be forgotten altogether, by the prehistoric cave dwellers, to the modern day setting of flora and fauna; immaculate.

Therewith; the human side of glorification was breathless. Leaving the earth as a better place when I died than when I was born. Just as I was fused and diffused by the buzzing sounds of the bees, as well as the buzzing sounds of my own confidence, and bona fide confidants.

Transfused by the deathless confirmation of the servants to God; all of us, cohesively, whether we liked it or not: All the way to the external *fields of the omnipresent sages. That's where I first met Miss Universe, and I felt my spirit coalesce with the beatitude of her pageantry, as well as the stingers of the bees.*

Omnia vincit amor—love conquers all.

For me, that was the greatest compliment in the history of the word amalgamation, *speaking euphemistically from the perspective of a self-assessed introvert. Who lived, loved, and was synthesized by the compost, as well as the subsoil, living and dying in the same century as embodiment and prosperity.*

Derived from the rich, friable soil; speaking of the loam, as well as the peat moss. Those were the amenities of the terra firma, where I was greatly suffused by the lore of euphemisms, and the pervading baths of metamorphosis, with an amplitude of demerit, infiltrating morbidity.

The Voice Dissipating More Rapidly

And so the hour glass ran out of sand with high heels of eloquent speech, including silky memoirs that were time traveling at the highest speeds of light, to the top floors of heaven.

Ensanguine; that was my escalator; when I was introspectively morbid by the metaphorical degrees of infliction, as well as the inbuilt physiology of the earth's humus, alluvium, even deposits. Figuratively, but literally cultivated with more than a trillion acres of subsoil, replenished with an equal amount of sovereign dreams, and an equal amount of life-providing topsoil.

Copacetic; the flower's essence, as well as the spirit; no longer waiting by the Pearly Gates of heaven; but consoling the ingrates that were going to hell. Reproofing the judgmental people that judged other people while they were still living on planet earth; when they were all imperfect human beings themselves; vainly.

Now it was their turn, as well as the dictators of the world, a far cry from the kindest people on earth that ever lived; condoned by the bees, as well as the wasps that were also going to deride them for stealing their bee hives, and selling their honey to the fiendish fiends.

For all of the money that made them rich, and all of the greed that made them powerful, now they were impoverished, with fly infested brains, and all of their ghostly bones. Dead and broken spirited, unable to purchase the most valuable commodities of the afterlife. Those were the ones that entailed the most forgiveness.

Timeworn

Ingested, those were my accolades; with a sliver of human kindness, which I tried to exemplify, even when I was metamorphosed from my original state of botany, into the horror-filled world of a human being that was always sinful, but always remorseful. Bloodless, that was the worst part of my legacy.

Now I am enthralled, but still I am free, greatly intruded; but still articulated with speckles of tepidity, as well as mosquito bites of extremity, sugarcoated by the kisses of the bees.

Prodigiously, it was all accepted, greatly appreciated; ingratiating myself with the four-leaf clovers of heaven; those were some of my best friends in life, as well as death.

Forever and a day, that's how long the Lord smiled down upon me, making it snow and rain by the endlessness of time and space, with a little girl named I Love You, with the Fondest Memories so that my spirit could reflourish itself under the boundless ceilings of its own guardianship.

Decidedly, that's when I saw her spirit spliced, enmesh itself with the spirit of Ditto, Ditto, Reiterated, and the definition of contradiction came together. That's when I fell in love, all over again, along with the components of comparison; making all of my dreams come true.

Then he forgave me for my sins, but only because I was able to forgive those that trespassed against me. Even the beetles and the rodents that tried to eat me alive, but I understood the concept of their survival and forgave them anyways.

Imperishable, that's when I discovered the art of imperishability, painting a portrait of forgiveness, as well as my own infinitude; with all of my tears, and what was left of my ear lobes, when I rejoiced with the bees and the insects, as well as the environmentalists in the cordial setting of botanical coronations. That's when I received my certificate of peace and tranquility, by the modulated paradox of flowery valedictorians that were speaking about heaven in general.

Extant or nonextant: from the age of provenance, to the age of subsistence, with a simulacrum of sovereignty for all of the red roses that resided on planet earth, and kept me company by the opera houses of The Twin River of Echoes.

Discarnate, as a demigod from the deification of mortals and mythological beings (part human, part divine, but mostly a morbid, introspective flower); *I was still salvaged by the prolix of salvation. Yet I was asomatous; desensitized, without a physical body, and without a physical reaction; effectually; ending my journey for sovereignty.*

Ubiquitous, several years later, on the anniversary of my death I was reminiscing. So I sent the earth salutations from the lectern of heaven, from the anthology of the Magnum opus, to the collected works of the pulpit, with discorporate flowers, including bodiless analects.

Eluding: of or relating to the fixation of decimation.

Dust to dust, roses to roses, commemorating The Sovereign Rose of Morbid Lore; sempiternal: *Ashes to ashes, morbid thoughts, and morbid memories; of introspective rose petals, as well as introspective bicyclists. May they all rest in peace; without a time clock, or the second hands of further judgment?*

I have climbed the highest mountains. I have committed myself to the highest pinnacles of sovereignty; as an equal, but unequal flower of the earth that once participated in the equivocations of life and death.

I am Svelte; The Sovereign Rose of Morbid Lore, and that's all that I ever will be; with a human cologne that validated my own existence, even when I died. I will always remember these seven little words...I Love You, with the Fondest Memories.

In omnia paratus, prepared for all things, all things change, and we must change with them. Said of spirit, mind, and body: *Effectuated; from whence I came, and to whence I returned; as the fruition of all the red roses on the same day that heaven consoled me with a great deal of sovereignty; and a great deal of interminable circumlocution that was always expressive and potentate. I am Svelte; The Sovereign Rose of Morbid Lore.*

About the Author

T ree Story was raised in the Pacific Northwest from the age of five. He graduated from high school in Oregon, RHS. Then he studied at Oregon State University. His first language is Spanish, second language is English.

Aside from his parents, Tree Story was raised with five sisters; akin to another sister that died shortly after birth. As well as two younger brothers, and many wonderful nieces and nephews, plus a large extended family. All near and dear to his heart. Forever in his thoughts, deceased or living.

As it pertains to literature: Tree Story enjoys reading and writing about fiction, as a general and personal preference he enjoys figurative speech, abstractionism, epic poetry, analogy, hyperbole, as well as imagery. Conjointly, with symbolism, allegory, metonymy, similitude and metaphorical writings (as in script, dialogue, diction, and / or lexicon).

Additionally, Tree Story enjoys intellectual, thought-provoking, and articulate stories with a strong spiritual and moral overtone. Primarily about morbidity, including but not limited to comparison and contradiction. About faith, as well as demonology and otherworldly possibilities. Also; documentaries, biographies, and/or human-interest stories.

"Memories never die, but people do.
As long as I am alive, I will always remember
you with the fondest memories."

~ Tree Story

CPSIA information can be obtained
at www.ICGtesting.com
Printed in the USA
JSHW051522140522
25847JS00001B/73

9 781645 595236